Saad Farage

Nejim.......Nejim

A Thrilling Mystery Novel About Iraq

www.nejim-nejim.com

Nejim........Nejim

Nejim.......Nejim

By

Saad Farage

Available in the United States by the Author
www.nejim-nejim.com

PRINTING HISTORY
First Edition June 2009

Library of Congress Catalog Card Number
2009906396
ISBN 978-0-615-30273-7

Printed in the United States of America

1

Nejim.......Nejim

Table of Contents

Preface   7

Chapter 1   10

Chapter 2   Moving Out   28

Chapter 3   The House   39

Chapter 4   The Hotel   61

Chapter 5   The Garden   75

Chapter 6   Umm Ali   86

Chapter 7   Fixing the House   98

Chapter 8   Water Hole   112

Chapter 9   The Fortune Teller   122

Chapter 10   The Spell   140

Chapter 11   Ghost of the Past   157

Chapter 12   Talib   166

Chapter 13   The Black Hand Man   174

Chapter 14   The Jinns   187

Chapter 15   Tanoor   204

Chapter 16   Mortar Attack   214

Chapter 17   Umm Ali & The Jinns   225

Chapter 18   Free at Last   237

A Glossary of Arabic Words and Phrases   249

Chief Characters   259

Baghdad Map   261

Iraq Map   262

About The Author   264

Special thanks to Mariam Khalaf for her insightful thoughts and help, and to Lulu for her inspirational memories.

PREFACE

In the tense of my life, I was mangled; I was ripped apart and stitched back together again.

"Do you know your name?" The doctor asked me.
"Yes, I do."
"Do you know where you are?"
"No."
"You are in the hospital; you were involved in a serious auto accident yesterday. The bones in your left leg are completely shattered, your right knee is badly torn and your right shoulder is crushed, and you have massive head and hip injuries." This was on April 14, 2006, one day before I was about to leave for Iraq again to serve for a third year.
"Mr. Farage; what do you remember last?"
'I remember the pedestrian green light, but nothing after that.''
"Can you wiggle your toes?"
"And your fingers?"
"Good."

The next day, a police officer came in to visit me. She said:
"I am the police officer who wrote the police report. I was in the gas station across the street at the time of the accident. I heard a loud bang, when I turned around I saw someone flying through the air. It was you."

The police report said I landed 58 feet away and that the truck driver ran the red light and accelerated through the intersection. Other witnesses said that the lower part of my left leg was almost severed, and my left foot was sitting next to my knee. I asked

"Was I conscious?"

"Yes you were; you were talking."

Thank you God, I have no memory of that.

Oh-------well those Jinns are back in full play again-------

Nejim.......Nejim

Chapter 1

I met Nejim when I was in Baghdad. He owned a small butcher shop at the end of the street where I lived for a short period of time in the second half of 2004. Nejim and I shared extraordinary experiences in that hot summer in Baghdad that rival many of the past mythical tales of this city. My sister's house was located in the Mustansiriya District, close to the main road leading to the northern entrance of Sadr City. The main road cut deep into a kind of no man's land forbidden to outsiders. In the old days, it was a new huge track of empty flatland stretching east until the horizon met the skyline somewhere far away out to infinity. Now, it's a bustling area with shops and people, making it a commercial district connecting the old parts of Baghdad to a less affluent city called Sadr City. In the past that city was called el-Thawra, then it gradually changed to Saddam City; but lately it had acquired a new name that had a flavor of its own. The city has quite a history behind it, which goes back to the late fifties.

Famine set in following the disastrous spring floods of 1955 and 1956. The two rivers, the Tigris and Euphrates, billowed out of control, flooding portions of Baghdad and most of the southern parts of the country. The entire southern population was uprooted and went on the move. Village after village and rice field after a rice field sat under water for a long period of time. It was an epic flood that devastated the country – and the livelihood of the southern farmers. The history of floods in this part of the world goes back to five thousand years and then some. Local people were forced to pack up and leave for a better place up north. They settled in squatter areas along the eastern outskirts of Baghdad, behind a Levee built along that side to protect Baghdad itself from flooding. The monarchy government at the time started building a low-budget housing project further east, away from the city, but before completing the project, the monarchy government was overthrown by Abdil Kareem Qassim. Qassim completed the project and moved those southern immigrants to their newly-established city, which he called el-Thawra, the city of the Revolution. Throughout the following decades, the city went through different phases and metamorphoses, from a hub of the communist party in the early to late sixties, to the most recent one – as the support base of the firry Shiite cleric Muqtada Al Sadr. The city doubled and tripled in size and population over thirty years, and the outskirts of Baghdad caught up with the edge of the city only to be separated by Qannat Highway, The Great Divide between two different worlds.

Nejim was part of all that and more; he had had his shop there for many years on the edge of the overpopulated Sadr City. His father before him owned the shop and the building. I found out later that he was a lion for his community, and his cause. He had a relentless desire to achieve his purpose in life. Nejim was a voice for those who could not speak for themselves; He was more or less the unofficial mayor of the neighborhood. He knew everyone and everybody knew him. He earned their respect with his graceful and reasoning attitude. His extended family lived behind the shop, right on the main road. He had more to offer; a cause that was embedded in him for many years, a lifetime struggle to fulfill a destiny that had survived throughout generations of his family before him.

Fate intervened to connect the two of us; I who had lived most of my life in the west, and Nejim, who had lived and worked all his life in Baghdad, right outside Sadr City. We were opposites in many aspects of life, and the way we brought up and carried on our lives. Although I was a Christian Iraqi by background, the similarities and differences between us were many and complex, an intricate tapestry woven into our fabrics. We both had very long traditions and histories in this country, and came from the very southern parts of the land, and its roots. Yet we were raised differently. That's the case with most Iraqis whether they are Sunnis, Shiites or Christians; Iraqis are amazingly diverse but somehow united in land and history. We have managed to live together for millennia; at times there were tensions that pulled us apart and glued us together in so many other ways at the same time. Those bonds were tested throughout history and survived the periods of adversity; now, it's time for testing these bonds again, while history and the world is watching us.

It was a real nostalgic moment when I landed in Baghdad for the first time after all those years away from my birthplace. It was Christmas day 2003. The C-130 military plane took us on a spiral, descent evading possible missile attacks while shooting flares on both sides of the airplane. Baghdad International Airport, BIAP, looked huge from the air, but we landed in a small patch of the airport and soon found ourselves taking a horrific convoy ride, speeding through Ameriya

District, the most dangerous section of the highway at that time, which earned the name Ambush Alley. Many of the attacks came from the densely populated parts on both sides of the roads. I could see why; the median was overgrown by wild shrubs and trees which made it a convenient place to "Shoot 'n' Scoot". The route to the Green Zone made us a moving target, with our convoy of brand new SUV's racing through the streets of Baghdad to our final destination – the Republican Palace. Once we entered the Green Zone we were safe. The Green Zone had well-defined boundaries, river on the east, main road to the north, open space to the west, and residential area to the south. Historically, it was the government district for many decades, going right back to the monarchy era in the fifties, when the king built his palace here. Later that palace became the Republican Palace. In the mid-sixties, the US built their embassy next to the palace, but did not have the chance to move into the new building. The diplomatic relationship between the two countries and most of the Arabic world was severed in 1967, after the six-day war with Israel. The old unused US embassy building is still there and has never been touched to this day.

On the road, my thoughts took me back to the day when I left Baghdad for the last time. It was August, 1976. I could see my father watching me behind the glass windows at the airport, waving goodbye for the last time. His eyes were filled with tears. It was the first and last time I saw my father with tears in his eyes. He chose that moment to show his emotion so I would not say a comforting word to him; perhaps he was uncomfortable showing such an outburst of emotion in front of his son. He wanted to share it with me in a silent way, as a last unspoken gesture of compassion and love. It was his last chance, it was our last chance. I could not touch him or say comforting words to him. Perhaps things had to work out in such a mysterious way to allow a rare warm moment between father and son. Years passed and I could not make the journey back to see my parents again. When at last I made the commitment to go back and see them again no matter what, it was 1986. I called my father to tell him that I was on my way back to Baghdad to see him and my mother. "No!" he replied;

"We don't want you here now." At first I could not understand his abrupt refusal. I sensed there was a good reason behind his emphatic negative response that day. My overdue trip to Iraq had to be postponed to an indefinite date in the future. It was a time of turmoil which had started when Saddam took over power and kept on going for almost three decades.

Later, I realized why my father did not want me back. It was during the darkest moments of Iraq-Iran War. Things were not going well for the Iraqi army, and any person of military serving age was being drafted immediately into the army. My dad wanted nothing to do with that for me regardless of my new US citizenship. Years had passed and I had gotten married and had children, while conditions in Iraq went from bad to worse, with the invasion of Kuwait and the ten years of sanctions. My feelings toward Iraq never wavered. I wanted my homeland to see a better day. I joined the Iraqi opposition to Saddam's regime and tried with some of my close friends to make a difference in our own modest way, trusting our belief in democracy and the will of people to govern themselves and choose their own destiny.

Now it was time for me to try to make a difference, to be part of the new changes and help in any way I could to move the country in the right direction. But things were not as quiet as we thought they would be. There are many bumps on the road, as we were to learn later.

Two days after my arrival, I was itching to go outside the Green Zone to see the Red Zone, as we called it, the real Baghdad, after all those years away. To me the "real Baghdad" was home. I wanted first to visit old friends and relatives, our old neighborhood and the house I grew up in on the other side of Baghdad. I got a ride to the Rasheed Hotel checkpoint from the Republican Palace, and without hesitation I walked through a maze of concrete barricades and rolls of Concertina barbed wire, and went into the outside world alone. I was a bit apprehensive when I saw the streets jammed with people and old cars, so unlike the ones inside the Green Zone , but there was no way I was going to turn around . I had made up my mind. The thought of turning back to the safety of the Green Zone did not even enter my mind. The street next to the checkpoint was filled with many of the people who were leaving the Green Zone after finishing their work. Now they were getting ready to go home; most shared a ride, others had their relatives waiting for them. I flagged down an old taxicab and told the driver I needed his services for the next three hours. I said,

"I need you for the next three hours to take me around on the other side of Baghdad. How much?"
"10,000 dinars" he answered.
"Very well," I said and took my seat in back. He took off, then after a couple of hundred yards he pulled over and said,

"Stadi, would you please come and sit in the front seat; you will be less conspicuous this way." As I sat in the front seat, he looked at me again and said,

"If I were you I would take off the cap, that way you won't look like a foreigner around here." That was the last time I wore my Superman cap anywhere in the Red Zone. I thought to myself, I'm only five minutes into my big adventure, and I've already made two deadly mistakes that could have cost me my life. I never told anyone at work that I was about to go out on my own to the other side of Baghdad. I don't think they would have cared much anyway. I was excited and could not put it off again, not even for another one day. I was like a bird let out of his cage. This was something I had planned in my mind for a long time. In fact my entire trip back to Iraq felt to me like a dream come true, and I could not conceive of myself being in Baghdad without visiting all these places I was about to see. This might be a risk too high for most to take, but for me it was worth every minute of it after all these years. I had waited for too long to be here; I was not about to be confined in the Green Zone – I wanted to see and feel the real life beyond those barriers, wherever I could set my foot down in this country. I knew I would feel that way as long I was here in Baghdad.

Twenty-eight years had passed since I was here last. I wondered how Baghdad was going to look to my eyes after all these years. For many years I had dreamt about this moment. I had gone over my first glance and my first step here, everywhere and all around, again and again in my mind. Would I be disappointed? I wondered; is she going to be as beautiful as I remembered her?

I had built a shrine for her in my mind, a shrine I entered whenever I needed the love and affection of a city that had lived in my mind all these years. I counted the streets and buildings and paced the roads and talked to the people, all in my dreams and even in my waking hours. Now I wanted to know how my city was doing. I knew she was going through hard times and might not look the way I saw her in my dreams, but I wanted to tell her: I am here. For me Baghdad began when I crossed the bridge and saw Tahrier Square, at least in the Baghdad in my mind. I was really anxious, desperate for the car to be on the other side of the river, waiting for my first glimpse. And I was there, almost there. The river looked different to me, smaller and hurt, and Baghdad was old and beaten. Baghdad was suffering and let down. But that did not bother me because I just knew there would be other times, better times, just around the corner. I noticed that this part of Baghdad had not changed much in the last thirty years, although the buildings looked older and in dilapidated conditions, and the streets were dirty, with mountains of uncollected garbage at some of the street corners. Some of the building fronts were charcoaled black, with no windows or doors, How could they have gotten like this? I wondered. I asked the driver,

"Why is it that some of the buildings are black and have no windows?" The answer came swiftly and starkly. The man turned around and looked me in the eye as if I came from another planet and said,
"Car bombs; that one here happened just yesterday." He pointed to a bunch of carbonized cars fused in a heap in front of a building. A shiver went down my spine at seeing the aftermath of a car bomb for the first time. I had seen it on TV,

17

of course; but seeing it for real in front of my eyes had a different meaning, a depth of feeling that could not be explained. I nodded my head and looked no more.

"You must be new here." He glanced at me. I didn't dare to reveal my true identity,

"Yes, I just got here from Amman; I have been there for two years." I don't think he believed one word I said. I didn't care either way. I was busy looking at the streets lined with concrete barricades; some were in front of important hotels and government buildings, others closing entire roads, forcing traffic to detour through side roads, or splitting incoming roads in two. I noticed all the old movie theatres were closed. I did not want to ask my taxicab driver why and have him give me another one of his puzzled looks. My educated guess was that all public gathering places were targeted by suicide bombers, and movie theaters, or cinemas as we used to call them, were among these many targets. When I was a young man I adored going to the movies, because they were my windows to the outside world. It clutched with a saddening throb at my heart to see them shut down like that. Nevertheless I was delirious with excitement. Baghdad had gone through a complete transformation, not a good one I am afraid. Armed men in uniforms were everywhere. Some manned towers on buildings; others at checkpoints carefully looking through every car, then waving at the traffic to move on. It was a shocking experience for me to see Baghdad the way it was. It was a city in moribund decay, but Baghdad has seen worse, and I was sure it would rise to its glory again. In the midst of my elation, I noticed the road that led to our old house. I was tempted to ask the taxicab driver to make that turn so I could visit my old neighborhood, or what was left of the place in my mind, but restrained myself and begged my indulgence and curiosity to be patient for another day. I promised myself that there would be more visits, and one of them would be to my old neighborhood.

I was aiming to see a distant cousin of mine, Lulu. Their house as I remembered it was behind the American Library in the old days. That house was no longer there; instead a new construction was in progress on the same lot. Then I thought of an old friend's house not far away in the same neighborhood. We pulled over in front of the house. My friend's son answered the door; after a brief introduction he knew who I was and told me that my cousin has moved out to a small house next to the old one. We drove back. The house was small and had a long driveway, I rang the bell and waited for a while with no answer, then I thought that the electricity might be out, so I knocked on the front gate as hard as I could and waited. The front door of the house opened and a redheaded lady said in a distinct voice,

"Mino? Who's it?" I noticed her right away. I shouted back,
"Lulu? It's me, Saad Farage" There was a pause. I just hoped that she would remember me after all these years, and then she said,
"Saad? Oh my God," she came out running, trailed by a small white dog barking hysterically. She examined me head to toe, and said,
"I don't believe it's you."
"Yes, it's me. It must've been – "
"Don't say it." She said,
"Yes, that long, how are you Lulu?"
"Just like the way you see me; I am fine." Her voice struck a deep chord in my memories, awakening many moments of the

past. I looked at her and could not believe that after all these years here I was knocking on her door and talking to her again. The smile looked the same on a face that had changed after so many years. I hugged her intensely and I wiped away a few tears, while that little Tibetan Spaniel dog was bouncing up and down, wanting to share these precious moments too. Lulu was a petite woman but full of energy, the world and its cares faded into the background when she was around you. She was a pearl, just like her name means in Arabic. Her eyes had a special spark of life. She was always on a mission no matter how small it was, and would not give up before she satisfied the driving intensity in her. Her sturdy walk served notice to those around her as she came and went. The dog, Mimi, seemed to be emulating her mistress, and had taken on some of her ways.

That moment reignited a wonderful close friendship that lasted my entire stay in Baghdad. Lulu was my inspiration, best friend and companion. She took care of me like a child, mending my thoughts and soothing my soul, and I loved the way she raised her eyebrow or burst in scolding tantrums at me for reasons I could never understand. In fact she was the only one who could do that without reaping the wrath of my bad temper. Her sisters would look at her and then at me, baffled by the indifferent, almost unruffled response she got from me every time she went off like that. And she loved every moment of it; it gave her some sense of control and power, because she was the only one who could do that and get away with it.

For the next two years, every Thursday night was at her house, come rain or shine. She gathered the family for dinner, her two sisters and parents. Her forte was cooking, and every Thursday she surprised us with her eloquent cuisine. Janan, her younger sister, was colorful and a woman of means and virtues, a master of her elements and strength, while the older sister, Lamia was content and quiet. It was a must for me to be there regardless of the trouble I would endure leaving the Green Zone. She would not understand and would not take "No" for an answer. When I bristled at an unpleasant comment someone made, she was there behind me, poking me with a gentle push that needed no words, but said "Relax". I often hear her voice in my mind screeching at me for trivial things I often missed. She later told me that when she was seventeen my sister wanted her to marry me, but it never worked out because we were too young. I wasn't aware of such a plan. My immediate plan was to leave, to set off on a journey of my own to the outside world like my parents did before me. A few months later I was on my way to the USA.

We had an Iraqi interpreter at work, his name was Emad. We became very good friends. He was a thin and tall man with a hook-nose and a very friendly face. He became my shadow; wherever I went Emad was there trailing me. Every morning he had to enter the Green Zone from checkpoint No. 2. He left his car by the checkpoint and hitched a ride to the palace. At the end of the day it was my turn to give him a ride back to his car. He knew everyone and almost everyone knew him. He had been a permanent fixture in the Republican Palace since the first day of the invasion in April of 2003. People came to him and asked him to run errands for them or sent him to Baghdad for shopping; he was a handyman in one sense of the word, a handyman not for his carpentry skill – of which he had none – but for his skill in doing these small odd jobs. He was always on the run, taking care of something for this Major or that Captain. Everyone wanted his help at one time or another, including me. He showed me parts of Baghdad I loved and had never seen even when I was here in my younger age. I felt safe driving around with him in his old car, beyond the walls of the Green Zone, visiting friends or just for a quick dash out across the river to shop for a few things, which I found very refreshing away from the monotonous day-to-day life inside the Green Zone.

Emad was an old hand around the Republican Palace; he had a very pleasant personality with a contagious smile that would never leave his face. He was a "can do" person and the word no did not exist in his vocabulary; although some of the time you felt that this guy did not know what he was talking about, this was irrelevant in a way.

I knew I needed to buy a car of my own. Hundreds of thousands of used cars were imported from European and Asian markets and flooded the streets of Baghdad, causing monumental traffic problems. The borders were open and laws were not enforced; almost everyone brought in a car from overseas. Even Japanese used cars were showing up in the market with the steering wheel on the right-hand side; special auto shops were opened to convert those cars and make them legal to drive in Iraq. Europe and Asia practically emptied their junk yards here, in the local market in Baghdad and other cities. Some even came sheared off into two halves; they were welded back again locally, often with two different colors and unpleasant results.

With Emad's help, I went around shopping for a car. I wanted a car that was popular and would not stand out among other cars. Most of the taxicabs in Baghdad were Opels, so I bought a hatchback Opel. This car was a very popular one in the streets of Baghdad; it cost me around $2,000, or in Iraqi lingo 20 Wareqa. Now I was free to drive around. Leaving the Green Zone was not so hard. I always left through the bridge checkpoint on the south side. Entering the Green Zone was a somewhat more hair-raising proposition, with guns pointing at me from all directions. I had to slow down and flash my military badge from a hundred yards away, knowing that I was in the crosshair of a sniper rifle at all times, a very eerie feeling. Then I had to wait for the soldier to wave me in. But once they checked my badge and saw that I was a DoD Federal Employee, I was free to enter.

I must confess I had a few scary incidents at the checkpoints of the Green Zone when soldiers or those security guards cocked their rifles and pointed them at me. These were perilous moments I would never forget. The feeling that I was about to go down at any moment made me think if it was worth it, taking this risk, but the next day I did it all over again. Some of those British security guards in Baghdad were the worst, arrogant and unprofessional. Others in Basra were far better, I think because they were under the watchful eyes of the British troops there. When I used to go to Umm Qasr for my regular meetings at the port, I had to take the C-130 to Basra Airport, and then British security would take me for the two-hour ride to Umm Qasr. I was impressed with their professional approach. They were waiting for me in three armored land cruisers. I never saw one piece of weaponry in their cars; they were there, but just not visible. The best security guards by far were the Afrikaaners from South Africa, true soldiers, disciplined and masters of disguise. They drove Iraqi-type cars like I did with no frills or overbearing displays of power. Every move they made was deliberate, calculated, and calm. They were not trigger happy like the rest, but resolute and ready if needed.

Just a week after I bought my car the suspension bridge on the south side of the Green Zone was hit by a few mortars, with minimal damage. A maintenance crew was quick to repair the damage and reopen it. That bridge was brought down during the first Gulf war and another makeshift bridge, next to the real one but lower, was built for traffic; this makeshift bridge was still inexistence and was being used to this day by the US Army. Often, I used this bridge to cross the river to Baghdad. It led to the affluent parts of Baghdad where there were shops and where my friends lived.

Since I made a point of driving around Baghdad, I noticed something odd right from the start; in a traffic jam people pulled over next to my car and asked me silly questions, such as how much I paid for the car, or asked me for directions to a very obvious location. At the beginning I could not understand why. I told a friend onetime about it. He said,

"Everyone has a value on his head. Americans and other foreigners fetch the highest values, and they are targets for kidnapping. Those drivers who pull over next to you and ask you a casual question, they are basically checking you out; they got the feeling that you might be a foreigner. They would listen to your answer and your Iraqi dialect and judge your worth for their wicked plans. From your answer they can figure if you were a foreigner or not. If they feel you are not local they can immediately corner your car and try to kidnap you at gun point."

"I must look different to them."

"Not only that, they can tell from the shirt you are wearing if you are not local, even from the way you walk, if you were in the street buying things; if I were you I would get a real good suntan. Try to roll down the windows and stick your arm out the way Iraqis drive – but that half-grey beard helps a lot, you're a hajji for them."

My cousin also told me that even the way I walked was different than those who lived here, more of a sturdy walk; I could not quite put my finger on that yet. But those drivers who pulled over next to my car had evil intentions. Baghdad became a lawless jungle, where everyone they did not know was fair game for kidnapping. They were nothing short of what I would call scouts, freelance spotters for the insurgents and al-Qaeda, looking for any person who could potentially be kidnapped. They were the eyes and ears of evil. Obviously, my answers were good and my Iraqi dialect was convincing, although my Baghdadi dialect is considered old and the local dialect has shifted to a mix of southern and Baghdadi dialects – but I quickly made up the difference. I might have raised an eyebrow or two, but I did not quite fit the bill for further hostile action, or I wouldn't be here today.

When I thought I had seen it all, another one of those unexpected bumps opened my eyes. Driving around Baghdad was an adventure; roadblocks were common things, forcing people to drive on the sidewalks and in ditches to get around them. The main crossroads had traffic lights and although they all worked when there was power, of course no one paid any attention to them. At each of these busy intersections there were one or two traffic policemen directing traffic; people paid attention to them, or else, they would stop the car and yank the license plates off, and leave the driver begging and pleading for mercy. My car was the best buy I have ever made, it was tough, small, fast, and had plenty of room. The car was easy on gas, which helped a lot because I bought my gas from the black market. I never stopped in the long gas lines at the gas stations; it was just too dangerous for me and a waste of time. I bought gas from street gas vendors – they were everywhere, mostly kids on the side roads standing next to huge plastic gas cans filled with gasoline, flagging drivers to stop. The gasoline was green, red or yellow. A green color meant Saudi gas, red was for Kuwait's, and yellow for domestic gas. They flashed hand signs for the price of gas that day. The plastic gas cans held four gallons, and went for anywhere from 5,000 to 10,000 Iraqi dinars; anything above 7,000 Iraqi dinars was considered high, being more than six times the regular price. Later, when I was ready to come back home to US, I sold the car for $2,400 and made a handsome profit.

Chapter *2*

Moving Out

It was sometime in the summer of 2004 when I moved out of the Republican Palace at the end of my job with the PMO as a Project Manager. When I arrived here in Baghdad I was excited about my assignment. Finally I had a chance to make a difference and be part of the reconstruction effort, rebuilding the nation. At the beginning I was in charge of the transportation sector, including rebuilding the highway networks and the Umm Qasr port. But slowly I realized the mission was getting nowhere except lost in the maze of the bureaucracy and paper shoveling of rival agencies encrypted in the minds of those who held the might and power. It was a frustrating eight months of almost minimal accomplishments laced with red tape and ineffectiveness.

I made a great effort to rebuild most of the southern sea port, Umm Qasr, Umm Qasr is located along the Kuwaiti border at the most southern tip of the country: a short man-made channel that boasts twelve sea-berths and out-dated Chinese cranes. I dredged the channel and furnished the port with a couple of new cranes for unloading ships. On one of my trips to the port, a US Army Major came in and wanted to show me something. We walked to the other side of the channel to witness an ongoing smuggling operation. It was a bunch of oil smugglers loading a small ship with stolen Iraqi oil right outside the port water channel. He told me that he did not have the authority to stop them; and even if he did they would find another landing area and continue their operation.

Then I was reassigned to a new project overseeing many of the works in Baghdad that needed to be completed before the departure of Paul Bremer, a Czar of ineffectiveness and corruption, with a lack of vision and understanding of what this country had came to in the last twenty years. We had two months to make a difference. The purpose of the work was to appropriate immediate work for Iraqis on projects that had to be accomplished in such a short period. The general consensus was that Paul Bremer wanted to maximize his accomplishments before leaving Iraq. He had extra money in his budget because the oil price was going up at the time. I argued that the most important work needed in the city was to collect the garbage that was piling up in the streets. Garbage was not collected and people were dumping the garbage on side roads and on the side of the freeways. The next problem that faced the city was raw sewage filling over and flooding the streets, a health and eyesore problem; also the streets were in terrible condition. I argued that fixing these three problems would have a great impact on the people in Baghdad; that it was a modest target with a working plan that could put unemployed Iraqi young men to work immediately, and which could be achieved right away, before Paul Bremer left office. When I came up with a working plan to do the job, with fixed dates and the number of Iraqi people that could be put to work, I was faced with a brick wall of upset echelons upstairs in the palace. I quickly realized that others in power had other ideas and the money was already spoken for, and would be dispersed in another fashion. Nevertheless, I took the initiative on one or two matters – achievements that I will be proud of for the rest of my life. One in particular was the discovery of the Saddam Revolutionary Court Archives.

I began to be skeptical of the lack of progress. Thousands of projects stayed on spreadsheets and never saw daylight. Every day these projects were diced and spliced in many ways and presented in meeting after meeting with no meaningful progress, while project budgets were burdened by the exorbitant costs of overpaid staff and security companies. I concluded that it was done this way by design, and by the hierarchy; of course, I could be wrong about that. Sometimes I thought, that's the way government bureaucracy works. Adding to all that the security situation was getting worse by the day. March 2004 marked a turning point. Violence accelerated in the Sunni triangle areas, and the battles for Faluja was underway and in full swing. The rising Shiite leader Muqtadda el-Sadr took center stage, rousing the poor Shiite population in those areas such as Sadr, Hurriya, and Shou'ella cities in Baghdad. I did not like what the country was going through; something else was needed, some ultimate form of sanity to prevent such madness, some solution I could not envisage. I could see where the country was heading and the signs were not encouraging. The lack of leadership and incredible political vacuum pushed incompetent head figures to the top, jostling for power using the old ways of intimidation and other lethal means. The mistrust between the various factions created a culture of violence and death that plagued the country.

Those of us who worked in the Green Zone were shielded from the everyday violence outside our small world, and could not comprehend what was going on around us. Most of the people who were working in the Green Zone never stepped out of their security bubble; they were glued to their computer screens, cranking up those spreadsheets in earnest and attending endless meetings throughout the day. Staff worked there for months in charge of multimillion dollar projects, yet never ventured into the outside world, or visited one project site location. It was just not feasible to make such trips under the current security situation. Each trip to the outside could cost thousands of dollars in security details. I on the other hand was fully aware of the reality in the streets as I crossed the barriers to the real world, the Red Zone, almost every day. I knew every pothole in the streets of Baghdad, the latest checkpoint locations and the security conditions.

Occasionally a few mortar rockets landed in the parking areas in the Green Zone, with no meaningful damage. In the first half of 2004, the Green Zone was relatively attack free from the outside. Many Iraqis were living within that area at the time. Makeshift shops were sprouting on deserted stretches of road, and restaurants ran by Iraqis were frequented by Americans inside the Green Zone. I noticed many looters were going around in pickup trucks, raiding abandoned government building that had been bombed during the war, and stripping them down to the bones; young men on motorcycles were roaming the streets of the Green Zone selling anything from DVD movies to beer. That spelled disaster in the second half of the year, when the shop strip and a main restaurant frequented by Americans were blown up by suicide bombers. The authority implemented new strict security measures immediately after these attacks and cleared the streets from those shops and peddlers. Many of the Iraqis who actually lived in the Green Zone were evacuated, especially the notorious Qadisiya complex, where many hoodlums and profiteers were living immune from background check and prosecution. It was like an underground society created for the whole purpose of profiting from the Americans in the zone. The remainder of Saddam's servants who lived around his palace transformed themselves into these blood-sucking operators. The two suicide bombings were an eye opener which quickly prompted changes in the security situation in the months that followed. Before, we believed that the enemy was lurking right outside our walls, but now the enemy was in within and among us. It was a sign of what we were about to see all over Iraq.

After leaving the PMO, I decided to stay in Baghdad while I was looking for another job with the many American companies working on the reconstruction effort in Iraq. Some of these companies were doing real work and I wanted to be part of it. By now I was an experienced Iraqi-American. I felt there was more for me to do, and I was needed in more than one way as part of the reconstruction effort, although the environment and circumstances were getting worse as the political and security climates descended to anarchy and lawlessness in the streets. IED's and suicide bombers became frequent around Baghdad and the surrounding areas. In one incident, when a car bomb exploded in Karada, I saw a pair of pants of one of the victims hanging on the electric wires in the street; it stayed there for months and no one bothered to take it down. Despite all the indications of increasing hostility, many giant American companies had arrived in the previous four months, to be part of the rebuilding effort. They were looking for Americans with local experience. I was the right person at the right time and place, but I wanted first to have a taste of the outside world – outside that bubble of the Green Zone – and live like an Iraqi, feel and be in the real world.

I knew what to wear, and where and when to go out. On advice from Lulu soon after I arrived, we went on a shopping spree in Karada District to buy me Iraqi clothes. The streets were dense with shops and curb stalls filled with imports that were forbidden before the war; now with the open borders with Iran, Turkey, Syria and other neighboring countries, consumer goods were flooding the streets and shops of Baghdad, mostly cheap products, but at the right price almost everything was available. I parked my car in a narrow street, and we went on foot with Lulu looking around for clothes. The shops were packed with all kinds of products. I bought common Iraqi clothes to wear, those clothes that Iraqis wear, local checker-type shirts were the standard shirts here, and several pairs of Chinese made pants; oh, and a pair of flip-flops. Out went my American-made Redwing boots and Dockers pants. I realized that wearing the right footwear makes a big difference here; people notice that kind of thing, especially in those troubled days. My American boots were not the kind of the street fashion you might find around town. Iraqis were amused when they saw foreigners wearing the red Arabic headgear, the Chiffiya; it made them stand out even more among the crowd, and brought unnecessary curiosity. I wore it only when I was in the Green Zone. Not many people wear them in combination with shirts and pants. I even bought a couple of Dishdash's but didn't dare to wear them in public; it just did not look right on me. My grayish beard was just right and added prominent stature to my local look. Older men have revered statures and were often called hajji out of respect.

By now I had mastered my disguise and blended in with locals quite nicely. I even adopted a nickname for myself. For people I did not know, I was Abu Wa'el. Here names give away your entire identity. From the name Iraqis can profile a person, ethnic background, religion, even the neighborhood you live in. I could be neatly profiled as an Iraqi Christian, but with Abu Wa'el as a nickname I blurred that identity; it was neither a Sunni nor a Shiite name, and was accepted by both sides, a common name but very authentic even among Christians. I tested my new nickname when I was introduced to new casual acquaintances. I must confess it worked fine, partly because people expected to hear a name as Abu something, rather than your first or last name; the last name was rarely used in the first time around of introductions, unless there was reason for further identification, but for an informal conversation Abu did the job just fine. That's the custom here. Even Americans get nicknamed by their Iraqi coworkers; they just can't get away from their old habits.

I needed a place to stay in Baghdad for the next a few months and I needed it fast, a base for me while I was looking for a new job. For now I checked into a local hotel for a few weeks, but above all I wanted to relax for a couple of months and get to know the real Baghdad and the people. I wanted to blend in, be one of the people and live the day-to-day life just like everybody else around the city. I was nagged by a feeling that I wanted to be absorbed by my surroundings, and absorb the surroundings into me. I wanted to be re-naturalized, and now

34

was my chance to do it, before taking a new job or going back home to the US. It was a nostalgic feeling; something was embedded in me and wanted to see the light, even if it was only for a short period of time. I loved being here again. Both my parents had passed away many years back, and my brother had sold our old house in Baghdad; since then he had left the country too.

I called my sister in Amman and asked her about her vacant house in Mustansiriya. She told me that their house had been vacant since they left the country four years earlier. She was anxious to find out the condition of the house after all these years, and wanted me to go ahead and check it out. I told her that I would do that and I would call her later on and give her a full report on the condition of the house. The keys, she told me, were with the neighbor across the street, Dr. el-Hadithi; he was a prominent doctor who had lived in the same house for decades. I remembered him from the old days. It was a nice neighborhood as I remembered it. My sister and her husband raised five children in that house after they built it in the mid-sixties. The neighborhood at the time was a unique one. All the people living in the street were doctors. They received the lands when the Medical Union Association offered a limited number of medical doctors a track of land at that time. It was a mix of people bounded by profession and not by anything else, like religion or ethnic background as it is now. Hadithi, Metwali, Hamadani, Najafi, Samerrai; family names of different religious backgrounds and others, among them my sister and her husband, Christians; they all lived there in harmony. They raised their families in that street for many years and had very close neighborly relationships with each other. The children were raised in a good and healthy environment, a typical sixties and seventies way of life, affluently middle-class, a reflection of all middle-class families in Iraq at the time.

While life went on in the street, new problems were brewing in other parts of the Middle East, and Iraq was not an exception; hostilities and series of political coup d'états meant that governments changed many times over, and brought upheaval to the fabric of the strongly middle-class society. Things were moving at a fast pace, and the political landscape was changing swiftly; and then came decades of wars and calamities followed by sanctions. The vast majority of Iraqis had no say in any of the things prevailing around them, while these events intimately damaged their lives. Now the same middle-class society shattered and dispersed – a fact vastly underappreciated by the Americans and the new political establishments. It had been the backbone in the fabric of Iraqi society for many decades. The same was true for the neighborhood where my sister had lived; it had been transformed to reflect the current social makeup of the city. People's liberal social attitudes, and openness of the sixties and seventies, were muzzled through fear of the new wave of Islamic fervor that had enveloped the Middle East since the beginning of the late seventies.

The year 1979 ushered in big changes in the political landscape of the Middle East. One dictator was overthrown and another one made his first appearance as a president. It began when the Shah of Iran was deposed, and Iran was taken over by the extreme Islamists. The Middle East was not the same after that moment. It was the beginning of turmoil and violence. The Carter Administration was short-sighted and was sleeping behind the wheel at the time. Iran should not have been lost. Iran is a major country in the Middle East, and was the cornerstone of stability in the Middle East, and should not have been allowed to be ruled by extremists. The US could easily have altered events and prevented the defeat of the Shah at the time, or at least transferred power to a new democratic government that was sympathetic to the people, and accepted by the majority. But that did not happen and history took a turn for the worse. The new Islamic government not only wronged the people of Iran and destroyed the affluent middle-class society there, but influenced the entire Middle East, and quickly started exporting their ideology and fanaticism to other countries around the region. This was a disaster for the history of the Middle East, one that will take generations to change. We reap the wrath of that mistake to this day. In Iraq Saddam was consolidating his power over the years by eliminating his rival Baath party comrades one by one. Finally he made it to the helm and became the president. It did not take him long before he plunged the country into disastrous war after disastrous war, until finally the demise of his regime came in 2003.

Nejim.......Nejim

Chapter 3

The House

It had been twenty-eight years since I had my last glimpse at this neighborhood where my sister used to live. As I drove for the first time in the streets, I noticed the main road had changed completely. Many small auto repair shops had opened along the road strip on both sides. The wide curbs on both sides of the main road had turned to open workshop yards and parking lots for many of these small shops, and as far as the eye could see the sidewalks were cluttered with junk cars and construction equipment. The traffic on the main road was congested; this was a main traffic artery to Sadr City and the surrounding areas. Flooded raw sewage spilled over into intersections of the main roads and close to restaurants and bakery stores, but that had ceased to bother any of the residents and shopkeepers; they just had to adjust to the new reality, and they did. They had to walk around the dirt, and when a passing car drove through the stench, people had to head for higher ground and keep off the street as much as they could; the pungent smell was overwhelming. I clapped my hand over my nose as my turn came to go through the puddles. I had to roll up the windows every time I passed through that area, and drive very slowly, or I would get dirty looks all around from people on the sidewalks. Once I get home I had to hose down the wheels from a safe distance.

People waited by the roadside of the main road to catch a ride. Minibuses streamed down the road on both sides; Kiayatts, as in Kia, and Coasterats, as in the midsize Toyota Coaster bus. The rides would go east to Sadr City and Sha'ab or in the other direction towards the university and downtown Baghdad. I was amazed by the hand sign language exchanged between the minibus drivers and the people waiting for a ride on the roadsides. Each sign had a meaning, for instance telling a passing driver where the passengers intended to go; this way the minibus driver could make a quick decision whether to swerve to the right and pick up a passenger or keep on going. As for the cars behind him, they had to anticipate his move, or perhaps read the hand signs too and stay out of the way.

As I turned the corner to the side road, I could see the street was filled with potholes, and right at the corner there was an old garbage dumpster that never have been emptied; occasionally people got fed up with the mountain of trash, dosed it up with kerosene and set it on fire, which made the endless overhead wires catch fire. The houses just like the rest around Baghdad, suffered from neglect, including the house I was about to live in for the next few months. They were draped with deep black lines, utterly obnoxious, adding a sad look to the already depressing feelings of the city. Many people said the garbage fires were reminiscence of the burning oil smoke when Saddam torched up the Kuwaiti oil fields in the first Gulf War, and later the burning oil trenches Saddam had dug out in a bizarre way to obscure Baghdad from the air. What a crock, I might add. Later, I heard, many people hired the fire brigade to hose out this despicable show of defiance to normality, but others resigned themselves to the hand of fate in this unknown way of life. It might have been an added step towards to a less ambiguous of way of living in this ambiguous land.

I parked my car in front of the house and went across the street. I knocked on the door and waited. Not long after, a well-dressed lady answered the door. When she realized who I was, she pulled the door back and gave me this deep look, then followed it with a pleasant smile. She had recognized me after all these years. She had the most wonderful garden, manicured into an amazing precision and order. We sat there reminiscing about old times. She kept the keys in an old envelope with my sister's name written on it; there were a few electric bills attached to the keys. As with many Iraqis, her children were scattered all over the world, one or two in England and the not so fortunate ones still trapped in Jordan waiting for visas to some other European countries.

"Your sister and her husband left four years ago to go to Jordan; since then the house has been unoccupied" she said.
"I know that. I hope things are alright in the house", She was silent for a while, then she went on, saying,
"The house was burglarized last year."
"My sister had mentioned something like that."
''Abu Sabah, the gardener "she said, "was supposed to keep an eye on the house but since the house was burglarized, we have not seen him in the house. He is somewhere around the neighborhood; maybe he is ashamed of showing up again after what happened to the house, he is an old man you know.''
"Oh, I will try to find him if he's around."
''We called the police immediately but they did not show up. We could see the people moving the refrigerators and air-

conditioning units out of the house and loading them into a truck in broad daylight, but we could do nothing about it, it was Hawasim", she added, this being the Iraqi word for the perpetrators of the looting that occurred after the war.

"When did this happen?"

"Last summer, almost a year ago."

"Is this neighborhood safe now?"

"It is now, but then, right after the war, those hooligans were marching through the streets looking for trouble and empty houses to break into."

"I am glad you are safe; it's so good to see you again."

"We are happy to see you here, and if you need anything please do not hesitate to knock on our door, we are here to help." I thanked her graciously for her help, and told her that I wanted to take a look inside the house.

I knew that the house was probably completely empty by now. Anyway, I took the keys and went across the street. It was a three-story house, two living rooms, a kitchen and two bedrooms and one bathroom on the first floor, and two more bedrooms, a bathroom, and a lower terrace on the second floor. The third floor had the highest roof top terrace, where there was a huge water tank. The front gate led to the garden and had an old rusted chain and a small flimsy lock on it. I opened the front gate. It was a typical Iraqi house, a fenced garden and a gate which had a long driveway led to the kitchen and the main house. The kitchen had a huge window overseeing the driveway and all the way to the gate. The house had big front windows covered by ornamented metal bars, as is the case in all Iraqi houses built in the sixties and seventies. It had a narrow backyard with metal doors which led to an alley right up to the front so no one would sneak into the backyard.

As I went inside, it was evident to me that the burglars had broken into the house by bashing in the metal bars on the front window in the living room. Some of the bars were sawed off, then pushed aside enough for someone small to get in and open the front door from inside. As I entered the living room, it reminded me of Omar Sharif when he first entered the winter house in *Dr. Zhivago*. The furniture was left as if time had stopped suddenly and people had departed in a hurry. The entire house was covered with a thick layer of champagne color dust, and not snowflakes as in the movie. It was telling a story of another time, perhaps a happier one, when joy filled the air. Like the people around Baghdad, you would notice a difference from the way they walk, as if they were carrying a heavy load on their shoulders or sometimes just waiting for a better time to come, which never did, so did this house – waiting for someone to come to the rescue. I was there and I was the person to make that difference.

Yet once I was inside the house everything struck me with deep emotion; all the electrical appliances were stripped from their places, leaving dark outlines on the walls and electric wires dangling towards the floor, except for an old TV set that was still sitting on one side of the living room (the poor thing was too old and too heavy to be snatched away and was left there alone to collect dust, fighting the element of time along with all the other debris). The front door lock was gouged out, leaving the door barely closed. In one corner of the living room there were stacks of long-play musical records from an older era. I wiped off the dust on one of them with my finger tips and took a long look at the titles. It was a stack of classics, Tom Jones, Englebert Humperdink and many others, mostly sixties and seventies records. Upstairs, one room was filled with medical books, tools, and equipment belonging to my brother-in-law, old and retired after long years of a job well done. Everything resonated inside me as I thought of my brother-in-law and his long career serving this country. He must have moved everything to here when he closed up his clinic, ending a more than forty-year career in his profession.

In another corner there was an old Singer sewing machine, a favorite for Iraqi housewives. My mother had one that she kept in perfect condition. I was in charge of hand cranking the machine when I was a little boy, while she meticulously mended our clothes; that old sewing machine had to be an antique by now, like everything else around the house. My thoughts took me back to those days, when we were happy and young, and this house was filled with the joy and contentment of a good life lived well. The house had fallen on hard times, but it could still be revived and put back together for me to live in for a while.

An old-fashioned dial phone sat on the table, untouched for years, a reminder of the old days; it was as black as a devil under the patina of dust covering it, too black for the dust to bother him. I unconsciously picked up the receiver, hoping to hear a live clicking, but there was none. I walked into one of the bedrooms downstairs; there was a big wardrobe stretched from one end of the room to the other. The drawers were pulled out and trashed on the floor. Many family possessions were scattered all around the room. The thieves had ransacked the room looking for anything of value; they left the things they could not sell – family photos, books, and other personal items. There were letters in one of the chests next to the bed. They were bounded with a yellow ribbon and put in a worn leather pouch. I carefully put the letters back in the pouch and set it aside for my sister. One day they will come back here, I thought to myself, and those letters among other things will be waiting for them, I will make sure of that.

No water, no electricity and no working phone; it was the same theme I had seen all over the city. Electric wires were strung up boldly around the house in despair, and a small electric water pump was still in the bathtub – an indication of a struggling time during the last ten years of Saddam's hold on power. A hole was cut in the window for a garden hose to the backyard faucet and the water tank above the house. I looked at the water pump and could not work out why it was there. Then it hit me; the bathtub was used as a water tank to pump the water up to the main reservoir tank on the upper terrace. They filled the bathtub with water first and then pumped it up to the upper tank. Out of desperation, people had to improvise to make ends meet; I saw the evidence of that everywhere around Baghdad and in the attitude of the Iraqi people. It came from a long period of deprivation; necessity took over in unimaginable ways to mend things and have them working, even for a moment, before they broke down again and the whole process was repeated all over in the same careful and patient steps. A set of oil lamps, Lalatt, was still sitting on the kitchen floor waiting for the dark lonely nights, while rattling windows added to the ominous atmosphere; good times, unhappy times, and now evil times yet to come.

The house needed a lot of work to put it back in livable condition. I had time on my hands, but did not have the people to help me out. I knew nothing about where and how to buy things. I needed someone who I could trust, so I could feel safe going out with him and being around him. It was not wise for me to walk in the streets alone. Some of these wise guys would spot me right away as a newcomer, just from the way I bargained on a price or how I asked for a particular item, and where to find it. I was always terrified of the thought that someone was going to come from behind and sink a knife in my side. When I did walk in the streets (and that was only under extreme conditions) I passed people with my eyes and ears wide open. Even with that precaution I was still vulnerable. All these thoughts were rushing to my mind when I was about to leave the house. I needed a local person to show me where to go and how to do things around here, someone I could rely on. While I was in the midst of my thinking I noticed a strange face was bobbing just above the gate line, looking right at me with a smile. Then I heard a soft knocking on the outside gate and this face was peering at me again when I opened the front door. He said,

''Diktor Saad, Dr. Saad.'' For people here anyone who came from the outside world was a Diktor, it was a matter of respect more than anything else; or perhaps I was a Diktor by my kinship to my brother-in-law who was one. I said,
"Yes" Then he said,
"I am Nejim, el-Ghassab, Nejim the butcher. I have a shop right on the main street. el-Diktor (he was referring to my brother-in-law) is like one of the family, he took care of three generations in my family and we owe him a great deal of gratitude and respect. We called on him in the middle of

46

the night when we had a sick child in our household and he never said no. He never accepted any money for his house visits. We don't forget.'' I thanked him for his kind words, and then he kept saying,

"I understand that you want to live in the house; whatever help you need comes from this eye and from the other one here.'' He was pointing to his eyes. I almost froze when I heard him, I was thinking to myself, words really fly fast around here. It hasn't been more than a few minutes since I got here. But I knew, that was the way it was all around Iraq, or the Middle East for that matter. First, I eyed him well, and with suspicion, but his serene smile kept shining at me. I wondered what else he would know about me! I was skeptical for a moment.

"What is your name again?"

"Nejim Diktor."

" Thank you, Nejim, for your offer; right now I am just looking around the house."

"Anything you want Diktor, I am at your service."

"Where is your shop?"

"Its on the main road on the left side. You will see the sign there. Come and visit me whenever you have a chance, Diktor." He kept looking at me as I started walking away, then something dawned on me, and for some reason I could not tell why at that moment and until this day. I suddenly turned around. Then I said,

"Wait Nejim, come inside and let's talk." As I turned around, I notice his eyes were alight with joy and admiration, and his face broke in a smile once he set a foot inside the house. I could not escape that moment, and I was not sure why I said that, and asked him to come. My throat was dry for a moment after I said that. It had happened to me in the past. As

47

if I was driven by other powers, and had no sense of control over what I said or did. But this time it was different, I felt that that was the right thing to do for reasons I could not explain; or was it? Something propelled me to talk to him and invite him in; even the words of invitation had a magic ring to them, and a real force behind them. I had to do it, but I did it with fortitude and gratitude at the same time.

I opened the front gate and let him in.

"Its been a long time since I have been inside your house."

"Yes, no one has lived in the house for a while."

"I love this house, and it means a lot to me to help you out in any way you want me to."

"I probably need your help; there is a lot of work needed here."

"Are you planning to live here Diktor?"

"I almost certainly will."

Nejim had this calm smile on his face, which put me at ease right away. He was a slenderly built man, medium height with stooped shoulders. His face had a dignified look, thin and unshaved. He had a small mustache resting above thin lip and a small mouth, and he had straight eyebrows and small eyes. His speaking voice was tame and soft, and he never allowed it to be louder than mine. He was wearing the usual Iraqi pants with a short-sleeve shirt, and a pair of flip-flops exposing thick soles going up the sides of his feet. What intrigued me about Nejim was his relentless smile and peaceful demeanor! Perhaps I wanted to know what lay behind that smile, or something else altogether, but I felt he was a person I could work with, and I needed someone I knew and could depend on in this neighborhood. Either way I was pleased for reasons I could not put my finger on for now; perhaps it was simply a matter of his simple and pleasant personality. But that was my opinion for the moment and it was not final; here people always had other hidden reasons when they were being super nice and friendly. I thought to myself,

"I needed help to repair the house and I need help now, yes that's it – and nothing else to it–". He carefully walked behind me, looking at the garden, which had turned into a small jungle with its shaggy foliage growing everywhere, and then walked around the corners of the garden as if he was looking for something, which I found very strange. He wanted to say something, but held it back for as long as he could. I stopped and looked at him, waiting for him to enlighten me with a suggestion or comments about the unruly garden, but he could not find the words to share with me, so I thought I needed to ease the conversation and open the door to his thoughts,

"Is there something wrong?"
"The garden needs a lot of work."
" Yes, I can see that, I am going to need someone to work on it." I said that to him and I kept going. I turned the water faucet, but no water came out through the other end of the garden hose. He lifted his hands up, as most Iraqis do as a sign of giving up, while he raised his eyebrows in despair. I turned around and kept walking while he was behind me all the time. Then he said,

"I have the right person for you to work on it."
"Who; Abu Sabah?"
"Yes, he is good."
"It seems nothing works in this house" I said.
"Diktor Saad, we will make it work."
"Tell me, how do you know my name" I asked? A minute had passed and no answer came out. In fact he lowered his

head, avoiding any eye contact. I looked again at his face, and realized it was too much to ask or perhaps no use to ask. I thought someone had divulged that information to him. The only person I had talked to so far was that lady across the street a few minutes back. But news couldn't travel that fast, I thought, he must have found up about my name in some other way!

We went around inside the house looking at what was left after the burglary. We were talking about the neighborhood in general. Nejim knew every family that lived there. He grabbed a piece of a metal bar and started poking the floor inside the house. I wondered what he was doing, but I did not ask him; it was as if he was looking for something under the tiles, buried treasure of some sort. Upstairs the door to the lower roof top terrace was open. The thieves must have used it and left the door open. Some of these empty houses were claimed by squatters after the war but, thank God, that did not happen here. I think it was something to do with Nejim; he kept a sharp eye on the place after the burglary and prevented that from happening. I was asking him about the burglaries over the last year and he said,

"Four houses were burglarized last year in this neighborhood. Right after the fall of the government, waves of hoodlums were roaming the streets and combing the neighborhoods not only here but all over Baghdad. Many people have left the country and left their properties unattended, and those thugs looted many of these houses and in some cases they moved in those houses and claimed them for their own. There is no government or police to challenge them." I felt that his sentiment ran really deep; it wasn't only

Nejim but most people felt the same way. The lawlessness in the streets right after Baghdad fell still exists to some degree until this day, creating an atmosphere of chaos and disorder.

The old neighbors, the ones who lived here for the last twenty years, grew older; some added new sections to their houses for their young children and extended families, but nothing was clearer to me than how life had changed and people had fallen on hard times. Their minds were static, and dormant from years of isolation and neglect in a world so dynamic it has no mercy on those who are left behind. It was a new generation of people here, a generation which had been left out and isolated; I call those who are under the age of thirty the Sanction Generation, wasted and uneducated. A generation left behind, with no skills to carry themselves through life. In contrast, my generation was different; affluent, upbeat and thirsty for new knowledge. It is a backward step that will need many years to be eradicated and replaced by a new mentality. Almost everywhere I went, I noticed the gap. People were disconnected from the real world, cocooned in years of despair and misery. Young men who could not read and write grew up with little or no education. Parents could not afford to send their kids to school. When those kids became young men they had nothing to do except carry guns and roam the streets.

Nejim said that this area was a sacred one and had long history behind it, pointing to the house. I was not sure what he meant by that. I dismissed it as nothing unusual because I knew that almost everywhere in Iraq was the same; you practically kick the dirt off where you stand and stumble on an artifact or two. Then he told me that this house in particular might be sitting on an unimaginable history. He did not elaborate any further. I knew that not far away from here, there were some old ruins. I could see many of the very old cemeteries and minarets on both sides of the Mohammad el-Qasim Highway on the way to here, so it was not a surprise to me to hear what he said. That's the way it was in our own small world here; unless he meant something more intimate or mysterious.

On the way out, Nejim took another crack at the water faucet again. The water came out gushing, bursting the garden hose and almost flooding the old row of roses. He took me by complete surprise. Before he left, he said,
"I was expecting you to come" I looked at him almost in disbelief to hear that and could not make sense of what he meant. How would he expecting me to come when he does not know me?
   "What do you mean by that?" I replied,
   "It's the house; surely someone had to come and take care of it. Those looters kept coming around and I had to chase them off; that's the least I could do for the Diktor"
   "But how did you know it would be me?" I asked. I did not get a straight answer from him. Again I asked him,
   "You didn't know me before?" somehow I realized I might be missing the point; there was more to the story than just that. But I left it like that, perhaps out of fear of not digging any deeper into it with someone I had just met. I knew the subject would come up again and that when he was ready he would tell me, and that no matter how much I pressed the point, I would not get a straight answer from him now.
   "Are you coming back tomorrow?" he asked me.
   "Yes, I will be here."
   "I can start making arrangements for the work we need to fix the house."

"That would be very nice; I will stop by your shop when I get here tomorrow morning."
"We can start on making a list of what's needed."
"Yes, we will discuss that tomorrow."
Someone I do not know was expecting me to come halfway around the world, amazing, I thought to myself. I gazed unblinkingly at him while he was walking away, I was too stunned by what he said and what he did, and dared not to move or think any further till he passed the corner on the way home.

As he turned the corner, I heard the water turn to a trickle and completely stop. I wanted to go back and challenge the water faucet again, but I was uneasy. Too many unexplainable things had happened and been said just now, today, since Nejim got here, leaving many unanswered questions. What did he mean by a sacred area and why he was poking the floor? Is he giving me clues to something? I looked back at the water faucet again and kicked it and waited for a miracle, hoping that this faucet might change its mind and give this thirsty garden another shot of water, but it didn't work. Strangely, I thought I scented a fragrant aroma in the air. It must be that the water put an immediate magic spell on the garden, a rebirth of some sort of these shrubs, the rose orchards, trees, and those awkward plants. They looked like reeds from the south that had migrated to here.
Global warming, I thought to myself; better than a misplaced tropical plant from South America.

I closed the door and drove away to uptown Baghdad, taking the Qannat highway along Sadr City. This highway had dips under overpasses and in these dips cars got disabled and traffic piled up unexpectedly. One time a dump truck carrying a load of gravel spilled his load right at the bottom of one of these dips and almost every passing car had a cracked windshield that day. It was another hot day here; the sweat was gathering on my forehead and coursing down to my neck, and patches of it were under my armpits. I could not wipe it off fast enough. I took a wet hand towel and at least a couple of cold water bottles with me whenever I left the house. By now I knew my way around through the main streets of Baghdad, or certain areas around Baghdad. There are places and roads there I would not dare to go to. Any wrong turn and I might end up in a big trouble. Some of these areas I wouldn't have ventured into even when I was growing up back in the old days, and now it was ten times more dangerous, and forbidden to the outsiders. But within the areas I knew, I was very comfortable driving around. I rarely stopped and ventured out on foot alone, or went on a long stroll in the streets alone. By now I knew all the shopping places, the good ones to buy my needs such as sweets; my favorite was one on Palestine Street called Saad's – as in my name – and another one called Abu Afif. I often stopped there on my way up to the hotel where I was staying, I stopped on Rubbayi Street to shop from the upscale grocery stores there too, or to buy a rotisserie chicken, which was very popular here. The best one was at Kehraman Square by the hotel where I was staying. I was thinking of food; I must have been hungry. Lulu's was the place for me to delight myself with a good wholesome meal.

My next stop was there for a cup of Turkish coffee. She had moved out to her uncle's house, next to her father's; both houses were located on a main road in the good side of Baghdad. This house was a lot bigger, with a nice backyard which connected to her father's house by a small inside door. I loved the laidback atmosphere there and the people that come in to socialize. When I left the hotel in the morning this was my first stop, or my last stop before I go back to my hotel room at night, but now I might have a house of my own to stay in for a while, at least after I had finished renovating it. My every day morning stop there became my daily ritual. The street was really busy in the morning and it was hard to find a place to park; this created an opportunity for Talib, a street vender who doubled up as a parking attendant in front of the house. He took the initiative and claimed that part of the street as his parking territory, charging people for parking their cars while doing business in the government offices around there. Once an empty space was available he enclosed it with an old spare tire so no one would sneak in on him and park his car without paying. At the end of each day, Lulu let him leave his cigarette and soda-peddling pushcart in the driveway overnight waiting for another working morning. In return he did some of the vegetable shopping for her when he was on his way to work.

There was always a guest or two in her house to hang around and talk about the current affairs in the city with. Her house was a hub for friends and relatives to meet each other and talk about the latest on the war and to swap that day's gossip. We have such a small community that is still alive and thriving here in Baghdad. I enjoyed the gathering there, and the special greetings I got from Mimi, her Tibetan Spaniel dog. A special breed even by US standards. She was Ms. Personality; she knew what was going on around the house at any given moment and was right on top of things. When I got there she would come and sit next to me as if I was her beau and she was proud to be in the spotlight. Mimi was a delight, a cheerful dog and a guard dog by nature. Her best spot was sitting in the front window watching life goes by. Although she was very small, nothing could stop her from challenging any intruder on her territory and what belonged to her, including us. She did her best to be intimidating, with serious posturing and sharp eyes on what went on around her.

Lulu's sisters came over and we sat down playing a game of cards. Janan, her younger sister asked me about the house. I told them about the conditions of the house and how it had been looted. They had heard similar stories before. It happened all over town. I told them about Nejim too, and his offer to help with the repairing of the house. They all agreed that I needed a local help while I fixed the house, and Nejim was the right person to do that. Lulu had heard about Nejim before from my sister but had never met him. She was interested to find a good butcher shop – which meant a lot for people here in Baghdad, and she thought he might be a good one. I told her,

"Nejim seemed to be a genuine person, but I will call my sister and inquire about him first."
Janan said, "He seems the right person to handle this work for you, especially as he is from that part of town, it makes a difference. If you think he is someone you can trust and work with, then I say go for it."
"I will see what my sister says about him first."

Something about him worried me, something unbalanced about the way he behaved when he was in the house; he was real curious, looking around as if he had lost something, and he made out of place comments about the house that I could not understand. I could not quite put my finger on it yet, or maybe there was nothing to understand. Lulu caught me gazing through the window, withdrawn in my thoughts, but she did not bother me with questions as usual, although I could see the yearning in her eyes. Perhaps she thought when the time came she would hear all about it. I learnt to confide my thoughts in her. She was one of the few people I could talk to and feel comfortable with.

"It's your turn" she said,

"Are you playing with us today?" Janan, the other sister said. She sensed too that I was swamped with my inner thoughts and not paying attention to the game. Then I noticed they kept looking at me and exchanging glances.

"It's your turn again." Janan impatiently said while she was giving me an intolerable look. I liked Janan; she had a zest for life and could be quite intimidating at times. Among the three sisters, she was the one who was swift and strong-headed in her thoughts and would not give an inch no matter what. But she could be very clear and right to the point.

"I guess it's my turn now." I dropped the cards on the table and told them that I was going to take a break so I could play with Mimi.

"Oh, you can't do that now, wait; I am about to finish anyway."

"Sorry about that, my mind is busy."

"We can see that, I hope she is beautiful."

"It's nothing like that. I am just thinking about the house. I

57

have to get on with refurbishing the house; that's what I was thinking about."

"So she is not so beautiful."

"You are trying to get me in trouble now Janan."

"That is not trouble to you. I am sure you can handle that."

"On another subject, I want to ask you something, since you know what's going on around here."

"I hope I've got the right answer for you."

"I want to ask you about the internet connection in the house. I don't have a phone line 'in the house." I wanted to change the subject anyway,

"You can get wireless these days, but it costs a lot."

"Do you have any ideas?"

"Yeah, there is high-speed internet but very expensive. It could cost you up to $600 to set it up, and $50 a month."

"Why is it so expensive?"

"They have to put an antenna tower on top of the house. It could be like twenty or even thirty feet high, depending on the area."

"That's not going to work for me, at least not now; I don't want to bring attention to myself in that neighborhood. I can't imagine a stranger like me moving into a new neighborhood and having a huge antenna on top of the house; it will raise all the wrong kinds of questions."

"Yeah, I don't think it's a good idea either."

"They will think you are running a spying communication network, you know how suspicious Iraqis are these days."

"Yeah, that big mouth gardener will be the first person to spread the word around."

"But if you have a phone line you can have a dial connection like the way we have it here in our house." In Baghdad there was a phone-dial internet connection available on renewable phone cards worth five dollars, each but I needed a phone line, which was not available in the house. The phone line was dead. I thought that was another item I needed to ask Nejim about tomorrow.

When the card game finished I was very tired. I retreated back to my hotel room, not far away on the river bank, taking side roads to avoid a notorious checkpoint at this time of the evening. I did not want to take a chance with those guys at night. When I got there the hotel was in absolute darkness; the generator was down. Oil lamps were everywhere in the hotel just like in the old days. That old generator broke down all the time; they have a person in charge of servicing it, but even with that it had more down time than the national power grid. I found my way up to my room. It was another hot night, with no means to cool off except taking a shower. I lay down, tossing and turning in my bed, drenched in sweat, thinking of what tomorrow might bring to me in Baghdad. I just needed to do without a few things and change my priority list a bit, and with some adjustment, I thought, I'll be doing fine. The only thing I can do is to hope for the best; things maybe are not as bad as they look, and there is always a bright side to everything, even around here.

Chapter 4

The Hotel

It was the next morning when I woke up in my hotel, Abu Nuas, right across the Tigris River from the Green Zone. A four-story hotel, it had a prime location, but was less affluent than the major hotels, which served me well at this time. I did not want to bring attention to my presence in a city that was filled with the eyes and ears of the wicked side. They could be anywhere and anyone, from the kid who is selling cigarettes on the roadside to the owner of a store in an affluent area. I had left the Green Zone a week earlier and checked into this hotel while I put the house back in order. I kept my distance from the people in the hotel and avoided small talks, which normally led to questions and answers. I maintained a strict Iraqi dress code. All pants and shirts including underwear bought locally, and I never entered my room without my Browning handgun wedged in my belt and covered by a loose shirt over the belt. I scanned the hotel for emergency ways out; it had an elevator that never worked, a stairwell, but also it had a fire escape stairs on one side. I knew I had very little chance to come out of a hostile confrontation alive. I knew if they ever found out who I was and where I was staying I might have a little or no time to pack up and leave. I was trapped in my room, but at least I would take a few of them with me. This moment was always on my mind, I had decided that the end would be of my own choosing and that ending was very real to me. It could be anyone of the workers in the hotel who would sell me out. I was a high-priced commodity and my head would fetch a premium price in the open market. That's how it was and I had no illusions about it. I kept all my personal papers and belongings in a black army locker, including my entire collection of American clothes, and my US passport, and I left them with Lulu. She was the keeper of my secrets. I hid my US army ID card either in my car or on me, because I did not know when I might need it to save my skin. It was a weapon with a double edge to it; it could scare people, but also it could be my downfall. I just needed to know when was the right time to use it or hide it, on the spur of the moment.

The scenery from the fourth floor was incredibly spectacular. I was looking at a nice villa across the river, in the Green Zone, and wondering. I could totally not place that building in my mind, mixing my old memory with the new one; I knew I visited a nice villa right on the river in the Green Zone a couple of times to meet a US Army general, but next to it there was something that caught my attention, a ledge protruding further into the water front, old perhaps, reminiscent of the past. I had the feeling that I was there once a long time ago.

I was troubled by the incident yesterday with Nejim; even more it intrigued me and raised questions in my mind. I thought, things happen because there is a reason for it to happen, and Nejim's case is no different. The things he did and said had their own reasons, and the answers will come up later on. My security was the most important thing I needed to worry about, and hiding my identity was top on my list even from Nejim, but he never bothered to ask me where I came from or what I had been doing in the last twenty years, as if he knew or that was not of importance to him. I set aside the whole thing in the back of my mind and went about my own business for the day. By now I knew where to shop for food and clothes, thanks to Lulu's guidance throughout the last a few months. We often went out buying things within their neighborhood, but we never ventured out beyond that part of Baghdad. It was time for me to discover the area around the hotel. This was the area where my dad had his clinic in the fifties and sixties, and my grandfather had built a house there some eighty years ago. My grandfather's house was no longer there. The site was not far away from the hotel on the main street. But things had transformed and changed since then; above all people don't look the same way they were before.

Two days before, I had walked to a restaurant a few blocks away from the hotel on the main Karrada road. The restaurant was frequented by Iraqi policemen. The place was packed with people at lunch time. The food and service were not so good and I decided against coming back again, and I am glad I did not go back there again. This morning, I heard a loud explosion, the kind that rattles the windows. I hurried to the balcony of my room and saw smoke billowing out in the distance, not far away from the hotel. I rushed down to the hotel lobby. Everyone was outside looking in the same direction. I asked the front desk man,

"Where was that? He replied,
"It's that restaurant where we get takeout food from." I
suddenly realized that I was there a couple of days ago.
"What happened?"

"A suicide bomber blew himself up inside the restaurant and took a score of policemen and other people with him." I could not believe I had been there in the same place; the streets were getting too dangerous, especially places packed with people and policemen. The safest place was home but I still didn't have one yet, that's why I need to fix the house right away and move in it. At least it would give me a sense of security in my own place. I was terribly rattled by this incident; it seemed that even the hotel was not a good place for me now. I drove by the restaurant, or at least the place where it used to be; it had turned into a grim charcoaled ruin. That was a near miss, I thought to myself. I could have been there. I wondered how many misses I was entitled to in my life.

It was sundown, and a mist of an orange bright light shone on the villa across the river, reflecting a dazzling display of lights on the water. I could not help but go to the balcony and then back, laying in bed again, looking at the ceiling fan, thinking of the old days. My mind was jumping from thought to thought. I gazed at the small white geckos; they skittered across the ceiling and feasted on flies and mosquitoes. They were doing a good job, stalking their victims patiently, and striking them with their long tongues at lightning speed. It was a good live show, rivaling anything showing on the Animal Planet channel. I took a chair and set it outside and sat there for the most of the night, thinking about the past and how things came around in full circle. Here I am again where I started, fifty-plus years ago.

I was born not far away from here, and when I was a child we used to dash out to the Tigris River for a swim in the hot summer afternoons. I knew the river then very well. The river bars where we used to swim now looked very different. Those river bars were gone and replaced by an ugly plant that was overgrowing everything. There was a villa across the river that belonged to the deposed Prime Minster Noori Sa'eed; I kept looking at it from my hotel balcony trying to see if that villa or a part of it was still there. The new villa could be built on the same location, but there was an old section that looked familiar to me.

"Could it be the one?" Then I thought, the old Prime Minster's villa used to have a sort of hanging garden extending into the river, which we occasionally used as a diving board to the deep water below. The new villa was probably built right on the site of the old Prime Minister's Villa. It must be – I was sure of that. When I visited the new villa, it had a magnificent river view. It was kept as a residence for the US generals here. I was fortunate to be there.

My friend Emad had got me an Iraqi ID Card and Driver's License to help me get around Baghdad. Baghdad was littered with police checkpoints; almost every couple of miles there was one. I was getting stopped all the time, but once they saw my gray beard and my Iraqi ID card I was on my way. My ID card served me well this time around when I checked into the hotel. I hid my real identity and made sure nothing related to my American real identity was left unattended in my hotel room. The people in the hotel were nice and had a huge electric generator, which was the most important thing around here these days. My room was on the fourth floor facing a busy side road leading to the Rhabat, nun, Hospital. Just across from the hospital there was an old church. This church was the place where we used to go to for a midnight Christmas

65

mass; they had the best Christmas carols then, some forty years ago, but now it was closed. I wasn't sure why, but it was the same story with the church in the back of it, where my aunt and her daughter were buried, God bless their souls; it was an old church too, and had a nice wood inlaid entrance inside and a beautiful altar.

Abu Nu'as was a waterfront road going along the river on the eastside of Baghdad, across the river from what was now the Green Zone. It was one of the oldest streets in Baghdad, but now it ended right there in front of my hotel. Further down the road was the Palestine Hotel where most of the journalists stayed; huge concrete blocks barricaded the road and the traffic had to make a right turn in front of our hotel, going through many twists and turns to make it to Kehraman Square. From there you could go north to Ferdous Square and the location of the infamous statue of Saddam, and south towards either Karrada District or the Rasheed Military Base. Abu Nu'as had seen better days; there was a time when the riverfront was the place to be for entertainment and having good times for families escaping the hot summer nights. Surely it had transformed since its heyday of this famous road in the fifties and throughout the eighties.

I grew up near Ferdous Square. That was the old name for the place, before it was converted to the monument of the Unknown Soldier. The square at el-Sadoon Street used to be a big patch of green grass surrounded by a real wide waterway circling the round square. As we went in the morning to buy bread from a famous bakery store, we purposely checked the south side of the circle to see if anyone had managed to cross the waterway overnight. That was the case almost every

Saturday morning. Patrons of Ali-Baba, a famous night club, drove down the road dosed up after having a wild night drinking Arack, the traditional Iraqi liquor, and raced through the street just before the big circle started. And guess what, there was always one guy who forgot to turn with the road. Some gutsy drivers even managed to make it to the center of circle.

Then, I was a five or six-year-old boy living not far away. One morning in July 1958, a historical day in Iraq, I woke up in the early hours of the morning hearing a loud sound coming from a distance. There was some commotion in the air, more noises in the street than I should hear on a normal hot day in Baghdad. I, as everyone else in Iraq, slept on the roof top terrace above the house, but on that morning of July 14th, the sound in the streets was something I had not heard before; it was the sound of military tanks moving towards the defense ministry. My Dad came back saying that this guy who lived two houses down the road from us called Abdel Karim Qassim was taking over the government. I knew the house very well, because so many dogs were there. Some said over forty. But I did know my dog Anter, an Irish Setter abandoned by his foreign owner when they left the country, used to raid the dogs in this house. I remembered onetime my dog went in and savaged two of his puppies. Qassim used to know my Dad very well because they both served in the same Army unit together, especially in the ill-fated Palestine campaign of 1948. He came in one day and told my Dad that both puppies had died. My Dad did not say much. I guess Mr. Qassim, or as we called him later "el-Za'eam, The General" had too many dogs anyway. But two more dogs weren't too many for him to lose. He was disappointed but my father surely told him it was his son's dog that did the mayhem, and he would not hold a grouch against a six year old boy anyway.

I went out to see what was going on. A big crowd was gathering in front of his house. Military people in their Khaki uniforms, wearing military Sedaras and holding small machineguns were everywhere. I had never seen so many soldiers in my life, except when my Dad took us to a military parade in el-Rashid army compound once to see an air show. I turned around and went back home looking for my dog. I was more concerned to see if we were going to play marbles that day or take out my slingshot and go bird hunting. There was nothing else to do since my dad hid my bike in the storage room, because I was riding it on the main road. When I got home my Mom was looking for me. She said,

"We are going for a ride." We all hopped in my Dad's station wagon, excited about the day's events. The streets were getting packed with people heading towards downtown. The atmosphere in the street was more festive, mixed with excitement, than confusion and confrontational. There was no violence in the streets, but it was more than enough for my Mom as she voiced her concerns; my Dad wanted to cross the new bridge downtown going to the west side of Baghdad. But my Mom vetoed that idea, and asked him to turn around.

"After all it will be more of the same, and we do not want to get stuck in traffic on the other side of town." she said.

"Very well" My Dad mumbled.

"I am hungry anyway," he said. My Dad turned around and we all went back home after he stopped to buy a newspaper and looked at the headlines.

That evening we listened to the radio. The King and his uncle were killed by the soldiers. Noori Sayead, the Prime Minister had escaped and everyone was looking for him; the new government and a huge street mob were on the hunt for him. It was in a sense a lynching mob, wild and unstoppable. I remember seeing the king and his fiancé early on that year in the military parade. But, I did not know who Noori Sayead was. That was until the next morning.

Next morning, the news came back that he was captured. Rumors said that he was crossing the Tigris River from his house on the river bank, which I think was where the present villa was located now in the Green Zone. He was caught dressed as a woman and wearing the traditional black Abaya. Later that year a related famous song came about called "Umm el-Abaya". That afternoon, Ali came over. He was a kid helping around the house doing few chores. I heard him talking to my Mom in the kitchen about what he had seen. Apparently he was telling her, that he saw the charcoaled body of Noori Sayead being towed behind a car. But as I came in, my Mom signaled to Ali to change the subject; it was a gruesome tale and my Mom would not let me hear it. The next few days went on as usual, except every morning and evening a big crowd gathered in front of the new Prime Minister's house. Some chanted slogans then followed it by bursts of clapping. It became a daily ritual. The little small store that we used to frequent as children was directly across the street from his house, a small store not bigger than a small room. That's the place where we bought marbles and celebrity cards. The cards came in small packets of crackers sold for five Feles, whereas marbles used to be ten for ten Feles. That was almost my daily allowance at that time.

My neighborhood was made up of two short streets connected by a small park. The little park was the place to play soccer every afternoon till sunset, rain or shine. The whole neighborhood stood on its own, with imaginary boundaries that could have existed perhaps only in a mind of a child. It was more so because for some reason it seemed that every family had a kid of my age, and most of us went to one of two schools, Adel or Sadoon Primary Schools; I used to go to the latter. The people living in the neighborhood were a true representative of the mosaic of Iraqi society , Sunnis, Shiite, Christians, Kurds, Turkmens, Assyrians, Armenians, Medians, and yes Iraqi Jews. Elweya ten years earlier was predominantly occupied by well to do Iraqi Jews. Many of the Iraqi Jews had fled to Israel in 1948, after their houses were looted. Only four Iraqi Jewish families were left in about forty or some houses in these two streets. Most of their kids kept to themselves, except Yousif, he was two years older than me, and the most savvy one among us, the most vibrant kid you could ever imagine, the best soccer player in the block. Yousif never wore a pair of pants, only pigmies and a pair of worn flip-flops, but he was everywhere all day till his older sister used to come to fetch him. She used to wait on the far end of the street and shout in a distinctive Iraqi Jewish dialect for him to come home. Most of the time Yousif ignored his sister and went about playing unbothered, then the second and third threatening shouts would come out from a distance, saying that she was going to tell her Dad. When his Dad showed up, Yousif knew he was in huge trouble. Sometimes we used to see him wandering around late at night, that is when he was scared to go home. He had to sneak into the house by climbing up to the upper roof terrace to get to his room, but the inevitable was always waiting for him in the form of a leather belt substituted for a whip.

Till two months earlier my best friend was our next door neighbor, Kamal. His Dad was the head of the higher Appeal Court then. I could swear that he was born at the same day I was, because we were so close, but his family moved out and I did not get to see him again till when we were 18. An Assyrian family moved into their house; their oldest son Alex was my age. Suran and Swara lived across the street. They were Kurds. Suran was one of the closest friends I had over the coming years. Later we learned to swim together in the Tigris River. There were other kids in my neighborhood, and I had a special memory of each of them in my mind.

After all these years, it was time for me to revisit my old neighborhood. I remembered it only in my mind as I rummaged through the fragments of the past. I wanted to see if it was still the same, but I did not have the courage to do so. I waited for the moment when I was ready, I waited for that self-intuition that comes from the inside telling me it's time now and I have to make my pilgrimage again to my roots, make that step to cross that barrier I had in my mind, a reluctance that held me back. I was afraid that I would destroy that image I held so dearly to myself. Every time I passed by the old neighborhood something inside me stopped me from making that turn. But one time I gathered all my courage and strength and I drove up to that road and parked my car at the end of that street, and I got out from my car and took a stroll in the old neighborhood. I hoped to see someone I might recognize, even a reflection of what I knew, a piece of those pieces I held and built deep down in my sacred memories that were so clear. It came back to me with a rush. I felt I was back to my roots again, where I grew up and where I spent my childhood, and close to our old house. I looked and could not see but imagine. The old house where I grew up in was no longer there anymore.

There was an ugly out-of-shape building in the same place instead. Even the building looked old and out of place, at least for me. But the rest of the houses in that street were still there the same as they were many years back, even the park where we used to play soccer was still there. It was a nostalgic moment. I thought of myself as the same old kid walking down the street, and forgot myself for a while. Things never looked the same as I had envisioned them in my mind and my dreams, still smoldering inside me. At the end I got in my car and drove away, not daring to change the images I had in my mind. I wanted to leave them untouched. I did not want to shatter my confidence and the colorful pictures I painted in my mind for all these years. It was better leaving it as it was so I could visit it again and again whenever I wanted, unaltered.

The hotel room was hot and unbearable but that's the way it was around here unless I lived in the Green Zone. I went over the day that had passed, what was done or left undone, and weighing my options to take on the task of repairing the house. I had a strong feeling towards that house, even though it was a bit far away from the safe and settled neighborhood where I grew up. The close proximity of the house to the hot Sadr City kept me wondering if it was the right thing to do. All indications were that trouble was about to brew in that city; and that it was bound to spill over to the surrounding areas including where the house was. But it seemed that I had a good help. I knew Nejim would do the right thing; although I was a bit troubled by his presence, I also knew that he meant no harm. He may be qualified as a peculiar character, but he seemed to be sincere and honest. Not many people around here would have that trait, of being sincere and honest at the same time. As far as his peculiarity, I thought I could live with that as long as it didn't make for problems. There was a dark side to it which might come up later, but as of now; he had made me an offer I could not refuse. There was no hope of sleeping tonight, waiting for the hotel generator to kick off while I was swimming in the dark and my own sweat. The circumstances called for a cold shower and cold beer, but even the tab water here was hot. I hated that old electric generator; the only place for me to park my car was next to it. In the morning my car was always covered with diesel fuel spewed overnight from that old machine; add to that the dust storms that were so frequent in the summer, and I had a gooey paste smothering my car. But I had to live with that as long as I was staying in that hotel. The Green Zone just across the river was lit like a Christmas tree, a source of envy to the rest of the locals on this side of Baghdad, those who did not have the same access to resources. Around two in the morning, the grid power came on and I managed to get some shut-eye for a few hours.

Nejim…….Nejim

Chapter 5

The Garden

The next morning, I made a call to my sister in Amman to find out if she knew Nejim and also to tell her about the house. I wanted to find out whether he was trustworthy.

"Nejim" she said,
"Yes, I know him. He is a good man. We have known him since he was a child; he grew up in the neighborhood. His father owned the butcher shop before him; now he is retired and Nejim has taken over. His family, and Nejim himself, are honorable and dependable people and you can count on his word, but above all they hold a great respect for my husband, who took care of them for many years. Nejim and his family never forgot such moments, when my husband woke up in the middle of the night and walked to their house to treat their sick children."

She confirmed what he was telling me about the old days. Nejim turned out to be a well-known person around that neighborhood; he was what I called the unofficial mayor of that area. My sister vouched for him and his good character. I told her about the conditions of the house and how it was burglarized. It came as no surprise to her; she was expecting that to happen as she had heard many stories of similar kind. I told her that the house needed a lot of work to put it back again in a reasonable shape to live in. I told her I would take care of that and would keep her posted on the progress of work. I felt comfortable now that I had someone I could count on. He had offered his help and I was happy that I stumbled upon him; besides, I liked the way he handled himself, and he was polite and well-mannered.

I pulled over into his shop in the afternoon. He had a couple of lamb carcasses hanging right up in the front, a deep freezer in the back and a solid tree trunk with a sharp cleaver sitting on top of it in the middle. On the side there was a meat grinder attached to a metal bench, and an old set of scales. On the walls were many posters of the late Sadr's grandfather, an Ayatollah who was executed by Saddam, and other posters of religious icons. Almost all the shops carried these posters to show their alliance to the new political powers now emerging in the country. Nejim was not there; another man was in the shop, but he seemed to know me well. When I asked him about Nejim, he said,

"Nejim went to the slaughterhouse earlier on this morning but has not got back yet." He was his helper and taking care of the shop while he was away. As I was about to leave, I heard someone shouting in a distance,
"Diktor....Diktor." It was Nejim, hurrying on foot after he got off of one of these minibuses. He was smiling and came running to greet me. After lengthy greetings that went on for five minutes, I told him that I had the intention to restore the house back again and live in it for a while. He was ecstatic to hear that. He reiterated his willingness to help in any way he could. I needed a crew of labors to clean up the house and the front garden, which looked like a jungle. He said he could

arrange for a crew and would go with me to buy the various things I needed. That was just what I wanted to hear from him; he was going to be a great help for me. I wanted someone to count on and help me around and he was just the right person to do that. He knew the neighborhood very well and he lived right at the end of the street.

I went to the house and opened the gate. To my amazement; the garden was in full bloom, enchanted by red and yellow roses as big as watermelons. Rows upon rows of mystical flowery combinations obscured the chaotic jungle order in a rare way. The two gardenia trees, my sister's favorites, had been given a total makeover and were full of white flowers dangling like chandeliers; some trailed all the way to the ground, where the light flickered on the petals. Even the citrus trees looked so healthy and green, I could swear I saw full size lemons as if they were the season's first, still clutching onto the trees even in this hot summer, and clusters of ripe October figs in August. All of a sudden the garden was transformed from a real jungle to a pleasant ornate bouquet, full of life and that mysterious aroma, blossoming beyond my wild imagination. It wasn't only me who was surprised by the sudden change; birds were flocking from every direction. Bees were buzzing around and having a wonderful feast day, sipping nectar from every flower, flowers that had not been there only this yesterday. The sound of other ungodly critters chirping endlessly on the trees made me feel at home. A pair of white-cheeked Iraqi Bulbuls showed up on one of the trees. They were chanting beautiful songs and inspiring melodies. Every couple of minutes they stopped and looked at me in a synchronized duet, then back to their singing harmony in perfect unison. As if they were greeting me with a nod of their heads between their songs or trying to ask me a favor. I looked at them in joy, a happy surprised smile on my face, as if I wanted to talk to them (why shouldn't I?); birds and flowers delighted in my presence and I did the same, as delighted as I could be with such a refreshing rebirth of life.

"Should I sing with you too" I wondered,
"Tell me, what's the special occasion? What are we celebrating?" I wanted to ask them.
Then one of them ruffled his wings and shed off a long white-tipped black feather from his tail, gave me a faint look, and both of them took off at the same time, swooping over my head again and again, and soared up into the sky. I took the feather and I slipped in my shirt pocket. It was meant as a gift for me, a delightful gift from two strange birds who displayed warmth and affection, gestures I could not find in many human beings. It was a sign of luck and good omen and I accepted it gladly.

I wanted to take a look at the backyard too. The backyard was a small stretch of garden surrounded by two neighboring high walls extended up to almost three levels. There was a high Nebga tree, a Jujube tree, like the one on the south lawn in Washington DC, overshadowing the entire backyard; it had a commanding presence. That tree's branches spread even to the next door neighboring gardens and trees. The Jujube tree in Iraqi mythology is known to harbor Melek, a spirit, and it is loved and revered at the same time. Neighbors would not dare to touch it or trim its overreaching parts. The rest of the garden below was overwhelmed by that treacherous plant from the south. When I took my first look at the backyard I knew I had a big job in front of me. I was sure I would not touch the

Jujube tree; she was on her own. She seemed in control of her domain. I did not want to have her wrath come down on me and the house, and would not want to disturb the Melek residing among her branches; he was my guest in a way. I had no call on them and would love to befriend them if that was possible. I whispered that to her when I was looking at her and I think she understood me very well.

Immediately after I arrived, Nejim wasted no time, he was right there at my doorstep with his unmistakable smile. He talked only when he needed to. The most striking trait about him was his calm demeanor, almost serene and quiet, and each word he uttered was followed by a soothing grin that never went beyond that. I noticed that he never laughed; laughing was unnecessary display of emotion to him. Between his smile and quietness I was very content with his personality. I learned to trust him from the first moment I met him, such a rare character in a world where trust could be the difference between life and death. Somehow I felt he had a hand in all this transformation around me. I waited to see how he would react when he saw the garden. To my great surprise, he did not even flinch, as if he was expecting what had happened, but he asked me if he could look at the backyard; once he saw the big Jujube tree he stopped and gazed at it. There was a screeching sound coming from the tree.

"What is that sound?" I asked Nejim,
"It's a tree cricket called Abu Feswa."
"They must be having a good time. I don't hear them anywhere else."

"They live on the fruit and leaves of this tree." Then he asked me if I had an Iraqi ID card. I showed him the one I carried in my wallet, and he said,

"Give me a couple of photos and I will get you a better one. The one I am going to get will get you anywhere you want around Baghdad except the Green Zone." I wasn't sure why I should bother, since I already had one. I asked him,

"What's the difference between the one I have and the one you are going to get me?"

"Diktor, there is a big difference; you will find out later on and thank me for it." Later, I fetched a couple photos and gave them to him.

We took a tour of the house. He had some advice for almost everything we saw, for him it came naturally but for me sometimes it made no sense, but I quickly learned to take his side and abandon my logic, because it was not logic over here. In many respects if I wanted to push my opinion over his, he would resign to the fact and say, Mashi, its Okay, but I quickly discovered it was not the way things were being done here. I had so many things to learn in Iraq. My main concerns were electricity, water and securing the doors, windows, and those holes that were left in the walls after the air-conditioning units vanished. Nejim had plans for those too. He wanted to put everything back in order. We had to hire people to do the work, and he took it on himself to do just that. He knew who to hire and he would take care of buying the materials too. I just had to trust him, and I realized I already did trust him implicitly.

I had learned to see things in black and white and right or wrong ways. A straight line with no curves and twists, this is the American way; it's been engraved in me for many years. Whereas in the Iraqi way or the larger Middle East way of things, there is a great gray scale area between the two, and there is a settled way somewhere in the crevasses between these lines. The lines curve and mangle together but emerge at the end in harmony after all the twisting and turning. It was there in palm trees and the words they wrote, that was the theme, not a straight line theme and no sharp turns, it was impolite and unacceptable no matter how wrong it might appear to outsiders. I had forgotten my roots. There was always a room to argue even when I thought things were already agreed upon. Promises are sometimes just promises because people would not say No in your face; it sounded unsociable to them, but they give plenty of body language with which they hoped to show you that they were not in full agreement with you. And people here had no concept of time; nine o'clock could be twelve or even next day or a week from now, and why not when nothing works and everything stands still at one time or another. Why take a sharp decision when the next thing you do is totally revisable and unworthy of the promise you just have made? We take basic things for granted whereas here it could be a monumental problem. When they didn't want to give you a time frame, they would say, "Inshallah" God willing, meaning time is irrelevant and things will get done when they get done. Almost every American worked in Iraq got frustrated with this word, and eventually learned how to use it in return whenever needed.

The jungle garden was buzzing with life. Strangely enough, the overgrown weeds and wild peculiar plants that were hard to uproot had an orderly pleasantness to them. I fiddled with the water faucet again hoping that it might work, but it didn't. I tapped on the pipes and even prayed but there was no mercy for the garden that day; but when I stepped on the grass it was wet. I waited for Nejim to try it, but wanted him to do it on his own way, so I waited for the moment to come. Then I thought the water faucet in the bathroom upstairs didn't work, so maybe he could direct his magic that way too. It did not take him more than a few minutes to fix it. I don't know how, and I didn't care to know how he did it.

"Okay, so he has his own ways with water and faucets, what other magic tricks did he possess besides fixing things – and – ? It must be wonderful to have such power, whatever it is. All will be sorted out, I am sure of that." I thought to myself. I have nothing against sorcery as long as it's used in a helpful way.

Nejim told me that Abu Sabah the gardener would take care of the garden but he might need help at the beginning. He said Abu Sabah is a real strange character, and later I learned why! He was slow but meticulously perfectionist, a treat here when things never lived up to your expectations. Sometimes I just sat and watched him working for hours. He showed up later that day and we agreed on a price for his work; as a goodwill gesture, I gathered some of the old clothes from the house and gave them to him. Patience had a whole completely different meaning here with him. I saw Abu Sabah working for hours on each rose orchard, manicuring each one at a time with tenderness and care. He never believed in using a mechanical mower; rather he was moving from one grass patch to the other in a squatting position, working his way around for hours, going on with his sickle and cutting the grass to a

82

perfect height. He gathered every heap of the grass he cut and took it to the dumpster at the end of the street. Every hour or so, he would get up and take a good look at what he had done from the corner of the house, and then he would go over the same grass patch and work it all over again. As if he was a painter looking at a portrait of his lover. I noticed he was avoiding one small area near the driveway. I was not bothered at the beginning and apparently he wasn't either. But after a couple of weeks that area stood out in contrast with the extremely well-maintained garden; I wanted to ask him but I knew he was going to ignore me and keep on doing what he was doing before. His drawback was his gossiping about the neighborhood women and calling them names; people tolerated him because he was old and good at what he was doing. He often muttered snippets of Iraqi wisdom that I had not heard of and I am not sure existed, except perhaps in the mind of Abu Sabah. As part of the deal, he expected me to prepare a lunch for him, and a nice full pot of tea and plenty of sugar for his tea break. Iraqis like their tea served in small glass cups and they drink it sweet, so sweet that it has to have a thick sugar residue at the bottom when they finish. He bitterly complained about the lack of water, but when Nejim left later that day, the water was running and there was plenty of it. At that moment it dawned on me that there was something special going on here with Nejim, water and some other things too.

I was curious about a new plant I had never seen before; it was growing everywhere, especially in the backyard. It looked like the reed bed of the southern marshes in Iraq. This plant had thick and dense roots and was hard to uproot. It could grow to six feet high in a matter of days. I tried to remove some of it using pickaxe and managed to takeout some of the deep roots, but when I returned three days later I saw it sprouting and alive again in the same spot. Historically, this plant is indigenous to the very hot and wet areas of Ammara and Nasirya provinces, and had never been seen up north as far as Baghdad before, but now things had changed – even the weather was a lot hotter. I asked Abu Sabah about it, and he told me to buy some chemicals from Batawiyin area, and he said it should burn it right off, but warned me not to touch the Nebga, the Jujube tree. I assured him none of that chemical would get on it. I made a trip to the shop he had recommended and asked for that particular type of chemical. It came in a brown plastic jar and smelled awful. I had to mix it with water and spray it on a patch of the plant, hoping that it would do the job. A few days later I took a look at it again, and to my great surprise the plant was as well and healthy as ever; it only smelled bad from the chemical. I gave up and left it up to Abu Sabah to deal with it; there must be something in the water that made the plant thrived in the backyard too.

Chapter **6**

Umm Ali

I learned more about Nejim in the following days, his gentle and kind side and also his dry confidence. Every month he went to the food distribution center in the neighborhood to help out the local officials and make sure everyone got their monthly share of food. Since the first gulf war, all Iraqis had been getting monthly rations of food consisting of rice, flour, cooking oil, milk, sugar and tea, and other food staples, a system called Hissa el-Tamwiniya. It was part of the sanctions legacy; what a miserable dark period it was in the long treacherous history of this country, a country floating on oil that couldn't feed itself. If anything good came out of that awful time it was this, Hissa el-Tamwiniy – how demeaning. But this is one program that has worked really efficiently in a country riddled with chaos and corruption. In fact during the Iraqi election, the Hissa el-Tamwiniya ID card was used to register Iraqi voters in 2005, because it was the most reliable form of ID. Many of the poor families lived month to month on their share of the food given by the government.

Nejim made it a point of honor that the elderly and the poor people got their shares on time around the neighborhood, regardless of their ethnic and religious background. He was there at the beginning of each month looking after those who had no other means of putting food on the table, and that day meant so much for them and for him too. He was well trusted among the people in the neighborhood. When people didn't show up to pick up their rations, he was there knocking on their doors to find out why and offer to bring it over if they could not make it to the food station. At the beginning of every month people lined up in front of the food station, and every month there was a surprise treat, sometimes in the form of an extra size of rice bag or flour, or other times a few gallons of kerosene when cold sets in. But the star of them all was the instant powdered milk made somewhere in a Scandinavian country. I had tested it at Lulu's and I must confess it tasted very good, a treat with tea and coffee, and made the best yogurt there is, thick and rich, rivaling anything bought here in the supermarket. I was hooked on that powdered milk from day one.

It was by accident when I stumbled on Nejim while he was on his way to one of these visits. I was on my way to the house when I saw him and his ten year-old son Karrar carrying grocery bags and going in the other direction away from the neighborhood. They both seemed like they were in a hurry and out of breath in a hot summer afternoon. I stopped and shouted at him,

"Nejim, I want to talk to you."
"Abu Wa'el."
"Where are you going?"
"I am on my way to visit a friend."
"Get in the car, I will give you a ride, it's too hot to walk."
He was reluctant at first to get in the car. But then he agreed.

"I am going to see a family in another neighborhood. I got some food for them; I picked it up from the food station."

"That's fine, I will give you a ride; it's too hot to walk in this afternoon."

"Thank you, Abu Wa'el."

" Who is this family if I may ask?"

"Umm Ali is a widow, she is a distant relative."

We drove to a less affluent area in narrow, twisting and turning streets filled with kids playing outside until finally we stopped in front of small old house with high walls. The rusty metal door looked more like a small fortress. Nejim stepped out of the car and knocked on the door, and two kids came over and greeted him. It seems they knew him very well. I could hear the door bolt pinged loud and then the door jarred open a bit. A lady, her face covered with the traditional Iraqi black robe, the Abaya, peeked out. The nervous look on her face quickly turned to a smile and the door was opened wide. He walked in with his son carrying many of the things they brought in with them, and then the door closed behind them. I waited in the car, soaked in my own sweat and wondering how long this was going to take. I had towels under me and on the backseat but even with that my pants at the end of the day had a big sweat patch. I wished I could wear shorts but that was not a good idea here; it was definitely not recommended.

After awhile Nejim came out, and asked me if I would like to come in. I walked into a place that I am not sure I could call it a house; there was an open small yard in the middle surrounded on all sides by rooms with no windows to close or doors to open, instead sheets or blankets were hanging where the doors and windows used to be. Small kids were running all over the place, mostly wearing rags and tattered clothes. A stack of pots were sitting next to a running water faucet on one corner waiting to be cleaned, and next to it a pile of laundry soaking in water ready to be washed. It seemed somebody had abruptly left his chore halfway through and hid somewhere in one of these rooms. Many of the clothes were still hanging on a string of line getting dry in this hot summer day. In another corner of the yard there was a small kerosene stove and Tanoor, the Iraqi round bread clay oven; among all this crowded mess, there was a small garden in another section of the yard, exceptionally well maintained, with roses that looked out of place in this house. There was a small empty birdcage that had no birds in it, but I could hear a bird or two making unruly noises somewhere around the house. I looked to find out where those birds were. I saw a couple of white cheeked Bulbuls there on an electric wire swinging cheerfully. I love those birds; in fact they should be the national symbol of this country. They always fly in pairs.

The lady who opened the front door welcomed me without looking me in the eyes, and the kids suddenly stopped playing and were gazing at me wondering in a very peculiar way. I could see more women were there in the rooms, peeking at me from behind these curtains every once in a while. The house was still and quiet. Nejim eased up the tension by saying,

"Diktor Saad, this is Umm Ali, Umm Ali and other families live here. I bring them some of the things they need every once in a while." The children went back to playing after this small introduction, but one of them leaned on her mother and clung hard to her black robe.

Nejim.......Nejim

Umm Ali welcomed me and asked me to sit on a mattress set on one side of the yard. Unlike most Iraqis, whose greetings may last for minutes or longer and sometimes stretch to a separate ceremony, Umm Ali's greetings were short and unceremonial, revealing some of her hidden character; she had a dry and hard look deep in her eyes, revealing an unyielding determination and strong will. She said a few words and showed a rare smile on an innately bony cheek. Her face and hands were dotted by seven Deggat, tattoos, on her forehead and nose, under her chin, and two more on each of her wrists. She had two gold-capped teeth on the left side of her mouth. I could see how poor those families were, and later I learned from Nejim that there were four widows living there with their children and two elderly grandmothers, in all six women and twelve children. Each had a unique shocking story to tell, but they had one thing in common – that their husbands tragically died and left their families in dire conditions. Some were widows of police officers who had recently joined the ranks only to be killed in suicide car bombs, others had their husbands murdered in the sectarian violence that was plaguing the city in the last few months. "But Umm Ali has been a widow the longest," Nejim whispered in my ears, while she was busy sorting out the foodstuff in the bags and preparing something to eat.

Nejim told me that Umm Ali sold her belongings one by one in the last five years, first the refrigerator and the gas stove followed shortly after by the furniture, one chair at a time, then the tables. Her son Ali had a pushcart which he used in the local market to carry goods for the store owners and earn a meager wages to help his mother and siblings. While she was making tea in the far corner of the house, I asked Nejim what

90

was wrong with the missing doors and windows in the house. He leaned back and told me,

"One day, Umm Ali was down to almost nothing and could not put food on the table anymore. She hung on and resisted to sell her last treasured item, her living room furniture. It dearly reminded her of good times when her husband was around and everything was plentiful and joyful. Those days had gone and the last reminder of those days, her living room furniture must go now. On that morning she pulled them out of the room herself, and told Ali to take them away. Ali came with his friends and took the living room furniture piece by piece to the main market along Muhammad el-Qassim highway exit near here. He waited for prospective buyers to stop and make an offer. When he could not sell the furniture the first day, he had to sleep on the sofa overnight and take the first offer the next day." I have heard similar devastating stories before, now I got to see an actual tragic one, and this one was the most distressing.

"When there was nothing left to sell, Umm Ali" he said," had to take down the doors and windows and sell them in the market for a scanty price, that's why they don't have windows and doors anymore." This was not an isolated incident. Many impoverished families did the same during the sanctions on Saddam in the 90s. It wasn't unusual to see doctors educated in US sell their medical books on the side of the roads around Baghdad."

"Soon" he said, "That area along the highway became an open market for people to sell their own belongings, you can see it from the highway as you drive on the northbound. The market had expanded since then." He added,

"After a while she took on other families in her household. Some of the women go to the market to sell vegetables in the morning. The boys help out too; some work in shops and restaurants as under-aged helpers and earn some money to help their mothers. The girls stay at home."

Umm Ali opened the food bags Nejim had brought in with him. Among the things Nejim had was meat from his shop. That was the only time those people got to eat meat, for them it was a luxury treat. She tried to prepare a meal for us. Nejim signaled me with the corner of his eye that it was time to leave. We got up and thanked her for her hospitality while she was protesting bitterly and insisting that we should stay for lunch. I was tempted to leave some money under the mattress for her, but then I thought, it would not be accepted and it might be taken as an insult. Then I thought, I better confer with Nejim first and figure another way to help her out. I was profoundly distressed. Now I had looked poverty in the eye. They did not even have one electric fan in the house in this hell-hot weather. I was profusely sweating in that house and I could not understand how those two elderly grandmothers managed to breathe, and make it alive from day-to-day in this hot summer.

"The children do not go to school anymore." Nejim told me; it's a luxury that they cannot afford, so they do without it for now until things get better. Widows with extended families to take care of are becoming another social burden facing the country." Many turned to begging along busy intersections in the city. As the traffic stopped, a flock of women and children would engulf the cars, selling anything from chewing gum to woven hand fans which Iraqis nicknamed in a sarcastic way; half a ton or one ton depending on the size, as in half a ton or one ton AC units.

We got up and said good bye to her. I did not want to shake hands with her because it wasn't customary to shake hands with a woman. On the way out, I saw him whispering to Umm Ali while she was looking at me, then she came and shook my hand heartily with genuine warmth in her eyes; I did not know what he said to her but it made a big difference and showed up on her face instantly. When we left Nejim said;

"Umm Ali's specialty is building those Tanoors, clay ovens, she is so good at it, she even built one for us long time ago." I said,

"I have not seen one in many years; I thought people stop using those longtime ago."

"Oh, no almost every household here has one to bake bread. Every month we receive a sack of flour for that." Then he kept saying,

"Maybe she can build one for you one day." Then he immediately changed the subject and did not wait for my answer. In fact I did not mind; I wanted to see how this clay oven worked. I could not connect her change in attitude with the Tanoor comment. But I was pleased to see a smile on her face and I was the reason behind that, it made me feel good although I was not sure why she had done it. Then he said,

"I hate pity, but I feel it's my duty to help out as much as I can." I tried to commend him on his genuine feeling, but I felt that he may not take it well, so I said,

"Most people do the same thing you are doing when they get a chance; it's very admirable of you to take care of these families." I felt that did not sit well with him.

"I am doing it because something inside tells me to do it."

"I know Nejim, and I am very glad to know that." He looked at me as if I didn't understand what he was saying. Perhaps I didn't, but whatever motivated him to help these poor families was quite alright with me and I was glad to see this side of him.

I asked Nejim if I could help in anyway, not as a show of sympathy, but as a human gesture or an anonymous caregiver. I offered to buy the children clothes and toys and asked him if he could deliver it to them in his next visit. Nejim turned around and looked at me, and then he nodded his head in affirmation, agreeing with no further comment, which made me wonder. It was a matter of dignity for him not to answer, and I understood him very well. That moment, I felt the power in his feelings. I quickly changed the subject to the house, but he was ahead of me and said,

"When we start fixing the house, I will have Ali and some of his friends on my crew to help out."

I said "that's an excellent idea," then I said,

"I will make sure that they get extra for a job well done at the end."

"Yes they would love that. It will be a great help for his mother and the other families there."

"That's a deal Nejim."

I began to understand the other side of Nejim. He was a kind and caring person and very respectful in the community. He often asked me about the US. For him it was another world, filled with lavish things and unimaginable wonders. I tried to explain to him how life is in the US in simple words, easy for him to understand. His eyes always rolled back in admiration and set him dreaming of the world he would likely never see. If he felt that he needed to disagree, he might quietly explain with great respect, how things are being done here. In a way we learned from each other a great deal. I assured him that although people do things in different ways, in a general sense we all share the same human feelings and in a way we all are the same.

Some of the things he said sounded bizarre to me at the beginning; they defied logic, but later they were reinforced by the reality here. That kind of reality made me also noticed strange behavior, as in people crossing the streets often looking in the opposite direction to the traffic, daring car drivers to hit them. Not only that, I even noticed that birds did the same, strolling in the middle of the streets indifferent of the cars storming around them and sometimes over them too. One time I hit the brakes hard to avoid going over a pigeon that refused to move over. I waited for her to cross the street and then I moved on. This recklessness was endemic in the country and spreading even to birds. I am not sure if it was a death wish feeling among some including birds too or living things just tired of living anymore. Nevertheless, it wasn't out of the ordinary in a country where everything was possible.

The new sense of freedom and democracy brought in mixed feelings and unruly behavior, while political powers jostled to establish themselves by using fear and intimidation and everything else at their disposal, disregarding the basics of the freedom they had just acquired courtesy of the US. Some misunderstood even the basics and violated the fundamental existence of human rights. It was going to be a long time before we achieved such a level of self-consciousness, but first we would need to work on the new generation and educate that part of society and dislodge them from the violence that was becoming the dominate culture and way of life here.

Chapter 7

Fixing the House

Inside the house, there was no refrigerator, stove, ceiling fans, and air-conditioning units, they were all gone. Almost all the electrical appliances were stolen, while some furniture was left there untouched. My sister had left some furniture in the house, of less value but enough for them to use if they ever wanted to come back again to this country. The missing air-conditioning units left big holes in the walls. Upstairs, the doors to the upper roof top terraces were locked, except the lower one that had apparently been used to move heavy items out of the house; my sister had left the keys hanging on the wall, but apparently they did not need them. The house had two levels of roof top terraces, as did all the houses in Baghdad. The upper level had a huge water tank at the top which served as a water reservoir, because water pressure is stronger at night and tanks had to be filled up for morning use.

The basics are electricity, water and security. But before that could happen, we needed to clean up the house, the thick dust almost like a mud cake that was covering the entire house. Dust storms ravage the country for days at the time in spring and autumn. The holes left open by stolen air-conditioning units made a great access to street cats that were running rampant around inside the house when I got here. One cat was in particular brought to my attention, she almost had no ears. I

98

could swear she looked like a wildcat, but her size was normal; she would never let me get close to her although she always sat outside the door guarding the house and waiting for a handout. She had deep gray and white colors and was well behaved. She was one cat that I let run freely inside the house. I wondered if her appearance was a freak accident of nature, or if she was just another victim of the circumstance here in Iraq.

Like anywhere else around Baghdad electricity, came once every four or six hours and lasted no more than two hours at a time, but during summer time when demands were at its peak, some areas suffered from ten or twenty continuous hours of blackout. Iraqis would say two and four, or two and six which means two hours of regular grid electricity followed by four or six hours of no electricity. There were times when electricity was out for more than two days. In a sweltering heat of 120 degrees people had no choice but to buy small electric generators which did not have enough power to run an AC unit, or in some neighborhoods the choice was to buy electricity from a private owner of a big electric generator, enough to supply ten or twenty households with power, for monthly dues. In our neighborhood there was one but far away, four hundred yards away. The drawback of sharing the generator was that it was out at midnight until six o'clock in the morning. If the Wataniya is not available during that time, then I will be on my own swimming in the dark for six hours with no means of cooling.

A good small electric generator would cost around $700, would be noisy, and would need constant maintenance and fuel. I could not see myself leaving the house in the dark at night to restart the generator, which was normally placed at a far corner of the house because of its noise. Many people got killed that way as burglars waited outside near the generator to ambush people in the dark, and the fuel dilemma had got worse since I arrived here. The gas lines sometimes stretched for miles; people would sleep in their cars overnight waiting in the line. But there were always those kids on the road sides selling gas for five times more than it was worth. I have watched Lulu spent half of the day driving around from one gas station to the other, and then when she got home she had to siphon the gas from the car tank by mouth for the generator, then run upstairs where they had the generator in the balcony and pour the gasoline in the generator tank, spilling the flammable liquid on her clothes and on the floor. By the end of the day she smelled like a gasoline station no matter how hard she tried to clean up herself up. I decided against buying one, and went along with sharing the local neighborhood generator.

Nejim took the initiative to contact the owner, and suggested to hire a local electrician to string up the wires. It was a monumental task; the line had to go over a couple of next door houses, then down to the street level and from there on going from one electric pole to the other, crossing a busy street at one time, which later I found was a big problem. My house was located on a side road, but it was not unusual to wake up in the morning to the sound of heavy traffic going through the street. It was often the case when the main road was closed and the traffic was diverted to these small side roads, and when big trucks started rolling down the road, they drove away with all the low overhead neighborhood electric wires.

Nejim came back with a local electrician to look at the house setup. He suggested stringing up two sets of wires going to the main generator on one end and connected to a changeover electric panel inside the house that he was planning to put in the hallway. The other electric line was connected to the national electric grid, which here was simply called Wataniya, National. The electric panel had a flip-up switch handle. Nejim argued with the electrician on what to use as an indicator when the Wataniya came on. Most people used a light, but Nejim insisted on a ring sound and two indicator lights, once the electric grid power came on, the light and a jingle sound would come on too, so wherever I was around the house I could either hear it or see it. In either case I would have to run to flip up the handle. Nejim thought that was the best possible way, and I had no argument with that. As the Wataniya normally came on for not more than two hours at a time, people rushed to run their AC units, laundry machines and iron a few shirts for the next day, then just as suddenly it would be out again. As I learned later, many times the generator owner forgot to restart the generator again, until one of the neighbors gives him a call or walked to his house to remind him. The system worked fine except when humans interfered intentionally or unintentionally and made things more painful than they were before.

We settled on a price, including stringing up the wires from one end to the other. The plan was to start the work in the next couple of days. I hoped that the electric power problem was settled for now, so then I had to tackle the water problem, but that was easier said than done. Those guys did not show up until the next week with a small ladder and bundles of wires. The wires they strung up were low, not even 10 feet high and sagging in the middle. Many neighbors complained. I had to buy the workers a longer ladder and redo the whole work all over again. The first day of service was interrupted for some reason. I went out checking on the line and found out that it was cut as it crossed the street. Apparently a fire truck yanked it off as it passed through the street. Nejim took care of that; he had a crew of people from the neighborhood helping him out tying up lines and splicing wires on both ends of the busy road. It was a sign of things to come.

Before Nejim left that day, he gave me my new ID card and driver's license. I thanked him and put them in my wallet. I soon realized the power of these new cards. The next few months while I stayed in Iraq, I was never stopped by a police checkpoint , not even once; it almost had a magic touch to it I could not explain. That new ID card stayed in my wallet and was never used like the one I had before. There was no reason for that. It had a baffling power that hypnotized policemen before even looking at it; just having it in my pocket was enough assurance for them to wave me off and keep moving on. After a while I was concerned whether that was a blessing or a curse.

Water came only at night or very early in the morning, but most people had a water pump hooked up right at the main line; without it, water would never have even reached the kitchen sink. Aside from the water pump, every house in Iraq had a water tank located on top of the highest terrace of the house which would be filled up overnight to make water available for the next day. Ours was rusted to the core and needed to be replaced with a new one. Nejim suggested having an additional tank at ground level and one water pump at the

main. I agreed with him, he knew what was needed here. I just
didn't have a clue. When I found that that old Russian water
pump still sitting in the bathtub after four years, I knew that
the water problem was going to be a major one to tackle here.
The old Russian water pump was running alright; it leaked
profusely, but could still run with enough noise to wake up the
neighborhood. Nejim told me that we had to get two new
water tanks. In Iraq there is a specialty market for everything;
the hitch was I needed to know were these markets are
located. Some were just a short stretch of road, no longer than
a couple of hundred yards, located on the outskirt of the city.
To fix my car air-conditioning there was a short line of shops
in Sadoun area, garden supply in Betaweyian, and water tanks
in Baghdad el-Jedidda; only locals like Nejim would know
that. So the next morning we went on a shopping expedition
from one end of Baghdad to the other. We started with the
closest item to buy, the water pump, in an area I would never
dream of visiting again. It was in the old industrial sector of
Baghdad. I drove down the road gazing mesmerized by streets
I knew when I was a young man. I had been through these
streets before but they did not look the same. I was drawn into
the images and thoughts of the past. It became a daily ritual
for me as I drove around Baghdad and met people I have not
seen in a long time. Friends got older and didn't look the same
as I knew them before. Simple things triggered a flash
memory in my mind, old buildings which were not so old
then, even windows and doors of old places still glued to my
memories of the past. These flash thoughts of the past had a
lightning speed and left me puzzled and delighted at the same
time, and sometimes had a feeling and taste of sadness to
them, mixed with fear and hope. What should I do about it? I
thought, "Should I muffle these images or let them out!" In

reality I had no control over them. They kept coming head on right in front of me whether I wanted them to or not. At the end I was brave enough to accept things as they were, as the natural order of things.

Nejim jolted me out of my thoughts.

"Stadi, we are almost there" he said.

"Let's find a parking space." We were on our way to buy a water pump, the first item we had on our long list to fix the house.

A young man waved to us to take a vacant parking space on the side. I swerved to the right and parked my car there, at a cost of 500 dinars paid in advance to this person who made street parking a new business for himself on this stretch of the road. We got out and went through a dirty alley that had small stores on both sides filled with cheap Chinese products and refurbished machines. Nejim knew what he was after, a small water pump which he quickly found, Chinese made. It was equivalent to fourteen dollars. We hurried back to my car hoping it was still in one piece which, surprisingly, it was, for thirty cents for parking that wasn't so bad. It was an area called Sheik Omar, an industrial area filled with old heavy machinery equipment and small stores that carry almost everything needed for people to go around fixing their houses and for construction contract works. Nejim wanted to buy two water tanks so he could put one in the backyard and hook it to the second water tank up on the top terrace. The way it was going with shopping, I thought we should have no problems with water.

We dashed across the town to Baghdad el- Jedidda. On one back road we found small shops busy making metal tanks of all sizes and shapes. The big ones were cubical in shape and the small ones were cylindrical. We bought two of them and had a truck deliver them to the house. That was a good accomplishment for one day. The challenge was to hoist the big tank some thirty feet up which we left to things to do for the next day when the crew would show up.

On the way back to my car, we passed through the bird market. They had finches, wild quails, parakeets, lovebirds, and canaries among other local wild birds. But I fancied a special bird. I wanted the white-cheeked Iraqi Bulbul. Just like the ones I saw in the garden. I know those birds can be tamed and grow to be one of the family. My dad always had one in our house. He used to let him out to wander around the house, until one day my brother left the door open and the bird flew out and could not find his way back home. The owner of one of these shops showed me many of them in a cage; he said "it's 5000 dinars with the cage for one of these birds". Then one person came in from nowhere and said,

"Stadi, I am going to show you the best singing bulbul you have ever seen"

"Yekhra.... Yekhra." he can sing.... he can sing. Then he showed me this bird. Nothing out of the ordinary. But the bird was so quiet, even the owner was surprised,

"He was singing just a minute ago, I don't know what happened to him," he said. I remembered the black feather I had from these two wild Bubul's in the garden. I still had it in my pocket. When I got the feather out and showed it to him, that bird went wild. He was jumping all over the cage and singing nonstop. That feather had a magic effect on this bird,

105

he must have recognized it for some reason I do not know. I said,

"I'll take him; how much?"

"With the cage 25,000 dinars" Nejim was standing on one corner of the store and quickly said,

"Take him" I looked at him, well he must be worth it, I thought. I said,

"You are the expert, sold."

So the bird came home with us. On the way back, Nejim asked me,

"What are you going to call him" I said,

"Sabr" Nejim jolted in his seat, I said,

"What's the matter?"

"Nothing." He said.

Sabr was a wonder bird. He must've had over one thousand tunes. He started at dawn and wouldn't stop till I fed him. He ate almost everything, but his favorites were cucumber, watermelon and dates. But he did not stop there; he was into white cheese and even chicken, which I found a bit distasteful, but he didn't mind. Fig was another fruit that Bulbul cherished, but I had to be careful with that, as the legend says the Bulbul invented alcohol; once the bird mixed water with an opened fig and let it sit for a few days and revisited again to sip the fermented juice. Then humans found out about this trick and got into making wine and alcohol. I did not want to have a tipsy bird on my hands, so figs were out of bounds for the time being.

The birdcage was made of date palm leaf wood. Iraqis must have been making the same design birdcages for thousands of years. Occasionally, Sabr took a bath in the water pot I left for him in the cage. He became a permanent fixture of the house; he even knew what tune to sing at any given time. At sunset he burst into a medley of songs, with a special welcoming tune when I arrived and another one when he was hungry or thirsty. I had to leave the radio on in the kitchen to entertain him while I was not around. He had a special why of greeting me, Lulu said,

"Before you turn the corner in your car, he goes wild and spreads his wings and goes on a special greeting dance. We know you are coming." Birds have a sixth sense, or at least Sabr did.

The morning came when Nejim arrived with a crew of seven, including Ali and another two of his friends. The first order of the day was a massive clean-up job. The houses in Iraq and most of the Middle East had tiled floors. Cleaning the floor is done by scrubbing and mopping the floor with plenty of water and some sort of local detergent meant for this purpose. But before they did that, they had to take all the rugs out and spread them outside for a later clean up. Once they did that, they started gathering up all the furniture and putting everything in the living room. I wanted them to clean up the windows first. The house had huge front and upstairs windows. The kids were working feverishly and by noon it was lunch time. I asked Nejim to get rotisserie chickens. They came with plenty of Iraqi round bread and pickles, and sometimes rice too. The kids had their fill, plates cleaned and fingers licked, and they washed it down with Iraqi Pepsi's. Around three o'clock in the afternoon, it was time for them to go home.

Cleaning and scrubbing was the order of the day for those kids for the next three days, while Nejim and I installed the water tanks and water pumps and other fixtures. We had to hoist the huge water tank all the way up to the upper terrace more than thirty feet high, and hook it up to a smaller water tank down stairs. We had one water pump by the tank to pump water up and a second one in front of the house activated from the inside. The water situation was under control and after several trial and error mishaps, water was pumping to the upper tank and all the faucets were in working order. We went and got bricks and cement to re-patch those holes left after the AC units were stolen. Nejim came back in the afternoon with a local welder to fix the broken windows and doors. Now I had the electricity and water under control, and I felt reasonably comfortable with the security situation once they fixed the windows. The house looked different now, clean on the inside, which was I all cared about. A paint job was in order, but I decided to leave that to some other time. The kids moved back the furniture to each room before they finished their work. I was generous to every single one of them, with a big gratuity on top of their regular pay.

Finally we came to the last day of work on the house. It was a job well done; everything seemed in working and satisfactory condition. I paid all the workers a heavy tip for a job well done as I promised them. Iraqi worker expect a gratuity at the end of his work on top of his regular pay. Traditionally you have to make a promise in advance that they will receive an extra incentive pay at the end so they can work harder. The way it works is that you haggle on the price of any service and then promise them extra if they do a good job at the end, that's the Iraqi way. It comes out the same. I sent the workers away and I sat down talking to Nejim.

I liked the house now; it was clean and hospitable, but still not ready for me to move in completely. I still needed to fit it with electrical appliances. Now it was time to go shopping for electric appliances, a TV set and satellite dish receiver, AC units and ceiling fans, refrigerator and washing machine, stove and propane gas canisters, and dishes and pots. I had enough furniture, there were a couple of sofas and a dining set, and in the bedroom a couple of beds and dressers and a huge wardrobe cabinet. Upon Nejim's advice we went to Beirut Street, not far away from the house. There were three markets for electrical appliances around Baghdad, and Beirut Street is one of them; the biggest one was in Arrasat, and the third one was in Baghdad el-Jidida. Air cooling units made in Iran were stacked up by the hundreds on the road curbs in front of each store, all sizes of electric generators made in the far east, and other electrical appliances and Satellite dishes. I wanted to buy all the appliances from one store, so we didn't have to carry those big items around.

Most of these electrical appliances were made either in Iran or Turkey. Some were of a very poor quality. The big item appliances such AC unites and TV sets were either South Korean or European made. The prices were very competitive and there was not much of a difference between stores. I settled on one store and purchased everything from there. A small Kia pickup truck delivered the load to the house. We also found someone to set up the Satellite dish and the AC units. By the late evening we had installed almost everything in the house, including the satellite dish. That evening we were able to sit down and watch TV. The satellite dish received more than five hundred channels from Europe to Asia and the entire Arabic world, all free. This was the symbol of freedom for many Iraqis; before, a house with a satellite dish on top of the roof meant jail time for the owner. When we finished working that day, I knew I had a place I can call home for the next a few months.

Nejim.......Nejim

Chapter 8

The Water Hole

By now my doubts had grown to become annoying strange feelings. I had experienced so many small incidents that I could not ignore. These incidents were mounting up and I had to take a good look at what was behind them. It was a curiosity at the beginning to me. I wanted to know how Nejim knew about me, but now it was more than that; I wanted to be secure and safe in my new place. If we were at another time and place then I most likely would have brushed it off and not let it bother my mind, but here it was a completely different matter altogether. I realized it took a lot of convincing for me to believe in such peculiar and odd deeds. Yes, probably it was not more than that, and I should not be wary about it. So he was at my doorsteps in a flash of a second! And he knew my name! He could have asked the lady across the street, maybe he was passing by that moment and saw my car and because of his inquisitive nature he wanted to know, then he knocked on her door to find out about the car parking here in front of the house. After all, he is the unofficial mayor of the neighborhood, right? And his job is to find out about any strange cars especially parking in front of a house that was left vacant by the owner a long time ago, four years ago! I tried to rationalize things in my mind, and up to this point I was not doing a good job.

112

Everything is ridiculously absurd. And what about this water thing and the birds and flowers? Water here was scarce. Water does not gush out in a drought time when there is a water shortage in the city, nor would it run from a faucet on its own when for days on end, water was not available in the entire neighborhood, not even at night. Those birds in the garden, I could swear they were about to say something to me. The garden itself was so green with unusual flower sizes; every plant in the garden was supersized overnight. Those two birds were almost talking to me and they were making human gestures, it was bizarre if not insane. Now I convinced myself of the madness surrounding me in this house. But it was a controlled madness, a madness of different dimensions. I felt that there was a magical hand in play plotting and steering it in ways I did not know and had never known or seen before, but I could not put my finger on it, I could not say with great deal of clarity there was something wrong here or there. It was not magic and if it was, what kind of magic is it? Magic is a strong word even in this old land, the land of strange tales of Ali Baba, Sinbad and One Thousand and One Nights. Magic is when I see a flying carpet hovering above my head or in the garden. That's magic. Just because I saw these two lovely birds trying to be nice to me that's not magic, Bulbuls can be tamed like parrots; is a talking parrot a magic wonder? I thought I was making too much out of nothing.

I was puzzled by what had happened to me and around me in this house, and when things didn't make sense to me or add up, I was lost and could not stop thinking till I found a solution or at least a logical explanation. But in this case I was sure that I was lost and without a reasonable cause for these unnerving coincidences. It was something to do with Nejim as

113

much as with the house itself. He held the secret; after all he seemed to know more about the house than I did. I was tempted to call my sister and ask her if she had seen peculiar things around the garden before, but what should I ask her? I did not want to sound ridiculous and paranoid, asking her questions about supernatural things in her house. They lived in this house for more than thirty years, but the house had been vacant for more than four years now and who knew what had happened in the last four years. I thought if I did ask her, she would think that the summer's merciless heat was getting to my head. I decided against that and decided to wait, maybe it was all about nothing and at the end I would be happy as Sabr and content as my earless cat here, and if I had a problem well, Lulu was always there to smooth things out.

On one morning while I was there, the next door neighbor knocked on my outside gate. That was the first time I talked to him since I moved in. He was shouting and waving in a frantic way; I thought someone had been hurt, but that wasn't it, he was signaling to me to come out. He wanted me to come out and take a look outside, pointing to something I could not see from inside the house. As I was walking toward the gate, I could see what the problem was. There was a big puddle of water right in front of the house. The water was spewing out near the entrance of the house and the garden too, and running down the road, almost unstoppable. It seemed it was coming out of a spot in the garden along the wall near the driveway in front of the house. I did not know what to do about it, I kept gazing at it hoping it would stop, but at this rate I didn't see that was going to happen soon. I asked my neighbor if he had any ideas, but he wasn't sure either,

"It must be a broken pipe."

"Yes it must be."

"But normally water pressure is so weak during this time of the day." He said.

By noon time, the puddle was getting bigger by the hour, flooding the street and causing traffic problems. Nejim came running up. I wasn't sure how he had heard about it. He kept staring at the puddle and had a really dreadful look on his face. He was very concerned in a way I had never seen him before. His calm and soft smile deserted his face and his hands were clenched in a very firm way I could not explain. He said,

"We have to contact the Belediya, the local municipality." I couldn't agree more.

"It must have been a broken water pipe somewhere down there."

"Yes, these things happen here all the time, everything is so old here even the pipelines." I told him,

"Why don't you hurry over there before the whole place gets flooded?"

"I will get a crew to fix it."

"Please do and hurry, take my car."

He got in my car and drove off. I watched the water spitting out as if it was a geyser. The entire garden was getting flooded by now and the street too. It became a spectacle for everyone passing by in the street. People started to stop by and look and wonder what was going on with the water again. I certainly did not want to bring attention to myself, the first question people would ask is who lives in this house now, from there on they would start poking around and spreading rumors.

Around two in the afternoon, Nejim got back with two workers from the public works department. Although it was their job to fix the problem, which I thought was more than likely a broken pipe, they wanted a great deal of money for their work. Under normal circumstances such a problem would take weeks if not more to repair without meditative incentives to do the job right away. But I am very sure Nejim already had greased up those two guys and promised them more money to come, otherwise they would not even have come. The two workers were middle-aged men, but there was something unsettling in their appearance. Even the look in their eyes bothered me and the way they walked too was not normal. After a session of haggling on the price with Nejim, while I was listening to their whining on the money, we agreed on a price of 50,000 Iraqi dinars, which is about $40. But before they started working, the water suddenly stopped. As if someone had turned off the faucet. Nejim was alarmed for a reason I did not know. Nevertheless, they dug up a big hole trying to chase the broken pipe. They soon were shoulder deep in the mud. I was watching them work from my kitchen window; by then the mess had attracted kids and grown ups alike. One of the workers shouted that they were hitting hard stones beneath their feet. He took a shovel and tapped on the bottom. It was solid ground below him. I could not help it but to stop them from going any further. Nejim got very restless when he heard that. I felt there was no sense in digging any further anyway, and asked them to come inside and have a cup of tea while I thought it over. No Iraqis would turn down a cup of tea at any time. I wanted to see if the water leak had truly stopped. We sat down to have our tea break while the two workers were going over some of the old plans they brought with them, and contemplating our next move.

"This is amazing!" one of them said,

"There is no water pipe showing on this plan in front of your house; not on this end anyway!" I looked at Nejim, I could tell from the look on his face he was very troubled, then he looked back at me and showed troubling anxiety. Nejim seemed to know something I did not know, he was nervous; even his hands were shaking in an irrepressible way and he was biting his lower lip.

"Let me look at the plan" I said. The water pipe was on the other side of the road, and entering the house from the far end of the house." One of them said.

"Well what is it then?"

"I don't know." The other worker said.

"You don't know? We almost are going to have a swamp in front of the house and the garden is turning to a small pond. I am about to bring in my fish line and try my luck here"

"Well, it could be a spring!"

"A spring! We are not in the mountains? All that water discharging out! It's unreal."

"I know it does not make sense, but what can we do?"

"Maybe it's an old water pipe not showing on this map."

"That could be the case, but you hit solid ground there, anyway we still need to find out, and the only way is to go down the hole again and check the sides, but be careful and don't get stuck in there and don't go any deeper."

While we were having this conversation, a kid came over running, Nejim said.

"What's wrong?" he said,

"Ammi, uncle, the water has gone, come and take a look at it." We ran outside. The garden was almost dry and the street too, except for patches of muddy slush here and there. The water in the hole had subsided to appoint where we could see the bottom. I asked one of the men who was looking inside the hole with me, he said,

"It was an enormous swirl turning around and swallowing the water and everything in its way down that hole. The hole got bigger and bigger like a big mouth of an unimaginable monster. The ground under our feet crackled. All of us just ran for cover when that happened, we did not want to get sucked in the hole with the water. The women carried their kids and hid behind the walls. It just happened so fast, it did not last more than two minutes, and it was over." I listened to the man tell his story, and then I took a look inside the hole, It was more or less like the workers said; stones were laid on the bottom, man-made stones and nothing else. A firm bottom not more than a few feet deep. It's like all these thousands of gallons of water were sucked back in the hole again, by the stones! The four of us bent over looking down the hole, mystified about what happened and not daring to move, except Nejim; he seemed fine and less concerned, and his jittery posture had suddenly changed. He was calm and undaunted about what had just happened. I was scratching my head and could see the rest doing the same. The rest of us were puzzled to a point I thought that something was about to jump out of the hole and grab us and pull us down into the abyss to meet some sort of alien creature or living thing. I quickly took a few steps back and so did the other men; they were even more worried than me.

"Well there is no broken water pipe here for sure" one of the workers said.

"Whatever it was, it fixed itself up by itself." As if this hole had a life of its own, or the house itself and everything around it has a life of its own. I am a geotechnical engineer. I know how soil and water interact. I know for sure it should not be this way and there was no natural explanation for this to happen the way it did. The two workers wanted to fill the hole back in again with soil. I wanted to make sure that they would not get sucked in the hole. I had just had enough problems as it was for one day. I did not want them to go down the hole again. It seemed to me that the sides of the hole were about to cave in at anytime, and those two guys would disappear with the thousands of gallons of water that went back in the hole. One of the workers attempted to climb down again in the hole when I yelled at him not to do that. That worker froze in his tracks and could not move. The wary workers shoveled the dirt back down the hole from the top while they were looking at me almost terrified and shaken.

When they finished they did not bother to clean up from the dirt; I paid the men and they were more than happy to pack up and leave this place and hightail it for home. I did not blame them. I looked around to find Nejim; he was gone and so was everybody else. I wanted to have a word with him, but apparently he sensed that and left in a hurry too. What kind of magic power had forced all that water back in the hole again? It would take a huge water pump to do such a job, like a vacuum pump it had sucked it all in. It simply seemed that the water came out and went back in before our own eyes as if nothing had happened. The street looked deserted, as if something dreadful was about to happen. I had the notion that a big monster was about to spring out of the hole and devour us. I closed the gate and retreated back inside the house. The street was almost empty and deserted, everybody went home thinking something awful was about to happen. I locked the gate and walked back to the house. I looked at my bird, but Sabr was as agitated as everyone else and not himself either; whatever it was, it seemed contagious; all of a sudden everyone around here was acting in the same cautious way except me.

I on the other hand was expecting the hole to burp, causing a large sinkhole to open up at any minute and swallow the house, the car, myself and Sabr, and half of the street for that matter. I waited in the kitchen gazing at the driveway for a while. But after a couple of hours, that did not take place and my dire expectation seemed less likely to happen. I was confused to put it mildly. I carefully stepped out to inspect the ground, looking with my engineering eye for cracks in the surface which meant the earth is not stable, but nothing was there. I tried my best to avoid glancing at the hole for fear of some sort of a final act of defiance that might consume my existence, but nothing like that happened either. I quickly went back inside, contemplating my next move. Somehow I felt that the little bird was aware of this predicament but he kept his silence and would not tell me. I was going to bribe him with an extra piece of cheese for him to nibble on, but I waited. I think he was smarter than that anyway.

Chapter 9

The Fortune Teller

I was suspicious of the way things were unraveling around me in this house. This hole that spewed water out just to suck it back in minutes was beyond anything I had dealt with throughout my career as a geoscientist. The mystery of water and indiscernible behavior of birds; even the plants and flowers in this garden troubled me, they grew overnight to giant sizes fed by miraculous water ingredients. But for a moment I wanted to get away as far as I could from here and rethink the reasons if any for this mystery of illusion and untold power.

I felt I needed a break. I locked the doors, said good bye to my faithful bird, and then hopped in my car. I drove off uptown to see Lulu, searching for a peace of mind from this delusional insanity. I dared not take another glance at that hole again. I felt profoundly worn-out today and avoided the slightest look in that direction and the evil surrounding it.

Every time I felt I needed a breather, Lulu came to my mind. I felt I needed a place with people to call home, and Lulu provided me with that place and feeling. Nejim had no words for me as I drove off; he had left in a hurry even before I paid those two workers. I did not want to stop by his shop; I was so disgusted with all of it. His strange behavior today was hard to explain.

When I got there, Lulu greeted me with a big smile on her face like she had not seen me in a long while, although I had been there almost every day in the last couple of weeks. She was bewildered to see the look on my face and knew something was bothering me. I know it bothered her seeing me unhappy and today was one of these days, but she kept her silence for a few minutes hoping that I would open up on the subject. She went around doing her own chores, and every once in a while she came in to take a peek at my face again, hoping that I would say something. When she couldn't wait any longer, she came back and stood in front of me and jabbed me with questions,

"You look like you have just seen a ghost." When she heard no answer back, she said again,

"What is wrong?" she sensed that there was a problem.

"Are you okay, you have been acting strange lately, are these workers giving you hell?"

"It's more than that." I answered back,

"Tell me; I am all ears."

"I cannot explain it, because it does not make sense. If I tell you, you will think I am insane" she looked back at me waited anxiously.

"There is something unreal about this house. A series of inexplicable events have happened since the first day I set foot in there." Now I had got her attention, she asked, "What kind of things?"

"It's something to do with water and the garden, even birds acting strangely, and this guy Nejim, the butcher, you know

123

him. He is a bizarre character, something about him is just not right. He seems possessed, as if he has control on things around the house."

"What does that mean? Tell me, what did he do?" she was getting excited, I could see that from the way she was sitting, unease and jittery, and she kept changing the way she was sitting and shifting in her chair.

"For example, he was right at my doorsteps in two minutes after I got there, he knew my name and who I was."

"Maybe he had talked to that neighbor, the one who had the keys, or your sister had called him."

"Yeah, certainly not my sister, I talked to her, maybe the neighbor, anyway."

"What else happened?"

"Well just now, I am going to tell you that, but I don't think you will believe me."

"Try me."

"This morning water was coming out from somewhere in front of the house; I mean it was flooding the street. We thought there was a broken water pipe somewhere or at least that what I thought, so Nejim went to the Baladiya to get help. The two workers dug out a hole to get to the broken pipe, but could not find one. It was solid rock underneath their feet, but water was gushing out anyway. Then the water was swallowed back in the hole again in a matter of minutes, more like seconds. All that water – and I mean it was like a small lake in front of the house, suddenly it was gone, even the traffic had stopped to avoid getting swept away with the water."

"That's strange; and what's Nejim got to do with all this?"

"I am not sure, I have the feeling he does, there were other incidents happened too, and he was part of it. Anyway, it may sound silly, but I do not feel comfortable with the whole situation. Don't get me wrong; I like the guy and he has been a great help to me. I just feel I want to stay away from that house for the moment."

"Why don't you stay here for a while?"

"I wish I could, but there are so many unfinished things need to be done there."

"You are welcome here anytime you want to stay, but I assure you things will get better – just give it some time."

"Thank you dear, I am sure of that too."

She knew Nejim by now. She occasionally came with me to buy meat from him for her and her parents. Then she said to me,

"It sounds like something from the movies. But things like that could happen here."

"Not like that! Anyway, it's not something I am used to."

There was a pause, I looked at her but she was still hoping to get a better reaction from me, then she said with great passion,

"I don't know if you believe in Fatahelfal, Fortune Tellers?"

I quickly said,

"Yeah, and what's that got to do with everything?"

"Well just listen to me for a second, and if you don't like it we close the subject and won't talk about it again." She looked at me with a convincing expression, trying to sway me with her words,

"I was going to say if you do, they can shed some lights on such mystery as you put it."

"No, I don't and whatever you have on your mind, it does not work and I will not do it." Then she said,

"I don't believe in that either, but consider this as a way of just having fun" I said,

"No, and that's that."

"They carry their own weight here and many people do see them just to seek comfort of mind. Some have real psychic power, don't laugh. I know what you are thinking right now, but some have amazing power."

"I am not convinced; I just want to know what all this has got to do with me."

"Maybe nothing, just promise me that you will give it a thought."

"Okay, I will."

"I know one but she lives in the old side of the town. I have been there once, and I have to tell you she was good. Let's go see her, shall we? It should be fun and exciting." I had never visited a fortune teller before. I did not know that they had ever existed in the real world, but apparently they had, even here. I thought doing such thing was totally ridiculous, but apparently some people still seek their advice, and Lulu emphatically believed in their powers, or at least the one she knew.

"Why don't you read my Turkish coffee cup instead and leave it to that for now; maybe we will save some money by doing that."

"Okay, why not let me see." She flipped the cup back and forth and looked inside trying to think of something to say, and then she said,

"Oh, my God, I can see streams of water, it's turning to rivers! Come and look, right here." She was pointing into the small coffee cup while jiggling it to make the lines shine as if she had solved the mystery of my life. I gave her one of my scorning looks and said,

"You are being fatuous, stop that." I took the coffee cup out of her hand and ran to the kitchen and rinsed it off.

"You see, I told you…water…rivers."

"Let's go out and do a little shopping, I need to buy some food and water, I mean bottled water." She grabbed her purse and was ready in two minutes; Mimi was jumping up and down and wanted to come with us, but Lulu pointed her finger at her and told her to stay.

We went out in my car to buy grocery from the Ammana Garage market area. They had many specialty stores carrying a variety of foods. I packed the car with groceries, including Sabr's special white cheese and water. We went down a small alley where there was a small store selling only cheese, a variety of local cheese stored in big plastic containers filled with salt water. No one can live here without bottled water. I was sick many times just because I used tap water to brush my teeth. I packed the car with cheese, water, vegetables and bread. When we came back, I said,

"Let's go see your fortune teller, on one condition. Don't let her know in advance that we are coming. Let's drop by unannounced and see what she has got to say."

"When do you want to do that?"

"Tomorrow morning, I will come to pick you up around ten."

"What is her name?"

"They call her Umm Murad, and she is blind."

"She lives in Fahdel; this is a rough neighborhood in the old side of Baghdad, have you been there?"

"Oh, yeah, some forty years ago, I used to know that area very well. I bet it has not changed much since then." I was momentarily lost in my old memories of that of that time when I was a very young man.

It was a daily chore then for me to dash through the allies behind these roads on my way to workout in an athletic club somewhere on the other side of the Fahdal neighborhood. We were two young men of seventeen. My friend and I could not miss one training day. The national competition was just a few weeks ahead. Every early evening we met at his house on the west side of Baghdad, then we took the bus right to the edge of the unruly neighborhood, aiming to take a short cut through this packed area with small alleys and solid walls on both sides; we were destined for the athletic club on the other end of this neighborhood.

The club with its meager equipment was a hub for all Iraqi athletes in Baghdad. The place was not more than a couple of acres in size, tucked behind rows of auto shops in the Sheik Omer area. When my friend showed me the way through this neighborhood, I could not believe that so many houses could be cramped in such a small area. Really, navigating through this neighborhood and making it to the other side on foot was a thrill in itself. Many times we missed a turn or two and ended up going in circles, only to stumble on one of the landmarks we had in our minds and pick up the trail again. The first week was a challenge, but later on we found out that each alley could be recognized by its "Shenasheel – a bay window sticking out on the second floor right onto the street.

There was one good-looking girl always sitting in one of these windows, which later became a landmark for us. It was obviously most recognizable to us. As we made that turn, somehow our legs got lazy and our eyes were transfixed in one direction, hoping to get a glimpse of the young girl behind the Shenasheel. It was one good incentive for us to make it through the training that year and win the national competition for weight lifting.

"Yes I know that neighborhood." I said.

"Do you know your way through that area."

"Oh, yes sort of." She nodded her head in affirmation, but I wasn't fully convinced. If I didn't know her better, I did know for sure that sometimes she gets ahead of herself. I asked her,

"Do you know someone can come with us who knows his way around there?" I did not get a clear answer from her, so I asked her again,

"Perhaps we should have someone from there with us." Then she said,

"Yes, I know a lady who used to work for us many years ago. She used to live there, but not anymore. I will have her come with us."

"I think that's a good idea; we can pick her up in the morning."

The next day morning I came in early for my Turkish coffee and together we went to pick up the other lady. She had lived in that section of the town but moved out lately. The three of us took a taxicab to the edge of the alleyways, after navigating in the congested part of Baghdad. The taxicab dropped us off right at the main road and from there on we had to walk in these allies. Fadhel has not changed much since my younger years in the sixties and seventies. The movie theater on the main intersection was still there but not in service anymore, and the small shops looked about the same but older. We went on foot from there on. After we made several turns and twists through narrow roads fit only for pushcarts and on foot traffic, we reached a dead-end alley of high walls on both sides and the lady knocked on a narrow metal door. I heard noises behind the door and a young woman's face peered from a small window in the door. She asked us what we wanted. The lady said,

"We are here to see Umm Murad." The sound of the door latches echoed like thunder while she was opening the door. The young girl ushered us in. Her ankle jingles were making a charming sound in every step she was making, adding an air of mystical rhythm, of harmony, to the high-walled house. We entered an empty room with arched ceiling, and a small thin window, enough for a glimmering beam of sunlight to shine as it rested on the floor on the far right end. We sat on a mattress set on a cold tile floor. The young girl then moved in the same choreographed steps and stood in a far corner as if she was trying to be invisible and hide herself in the dark. She was wearing the traditional long black gown and black headscarf lined by another white scarf tucked tightly around her cheeks. Lulu and the lady sat uncomfortably on the mattress next to me. The room was almost bare except for a couple of oil lamps and the smell of burning incense. I could not tell where it was coming from but I could see the shadow of its haze as it crossed the sunlight path on my right. The light of the flickering oil lamps shaded dark lines on our faces. I could see the shadow of my face in the small mirrors behind each of these oil lamps. While we sat there, we stayed real quiet waiting for Umm Murad to make her grand entrance.

Minutes had passed and we were sitting there, not even daring to look at or talk to each other in that almost dark room. Then a pudgy old woman in black entered the room. There was no traditional greeting ceremony. Lulu tried to open her mouth but the words did not come out right, so she sat as quiet as she could be. The serious look on Umm Murad's face showed that she was all business. She immediately focused her blind eyes on me. She sat on another mattress across from me. She put a piece of red cloth in front of me and threw bunch of beads on it and asked me to pick them up and throw them again on that piece of cloth seven times. Every time she felt the beads with her hand she whispered words we could not understand, as if she was speaking in tongues. She was swaying back and forth as she was mumbling these words. We waited patiently for her to finish. Then she said,

"I feel the presence of the Jinns among us now. They are telling me that you had an unfortunate incident yesterday?" I could feel the two ladies sitting next to me getting a bit restive and uncomfortable, so I said,

"Yes, that's true." Then she went through another moment of silence, and finally said,

"Was it in your house?" I looked at Lulu; she was bristling with fear.

"Yes it was."

"This is a matter of utmost seriousness."

"I know; that's why I am here to seek your advice."

"What do you want to know?" I leaned back a little and looked at her dark stained hand squeezing the beads, I wasn't sure what she meant by that,

"I want to know why these things happened to me."

131

"Things happened because that's the way it was supposed to happen. You have to be patient and not upset the Jinns."

"I hope I am a patient man, and anyway why would I upset the Jinns?" I wasn't sure whether or not I would want to upset the Jinns, but felt I should play along and see what else she had to say,

"There are Jinns who want to help you and others want to hurt you, but everything will be revealed to you in due time. Your house holds a secret. The person who cares for you the most will answer these questions. You have to trust him. But do not be afraid, things will be alright at the end."

"Are more of these unusual things going to happen in the house?"

"This is just the beginning." Then all of the sudden she was rumbling and shaking while reciting religious phrases. The oil lamp light dimmed. The girl in the corner hurried towards her mistress and helped her to get up on her feet, and both of them exited the room and shut the door behind them. We could hear noises in the hallway, which then turned to whispering. We were looking at each other but we kept our silence. After a while the young woman came back in, and said,

"I am sorry Umm Murad is not feeling well, but she wants you to take these." She had seven rolled pieces of papers and seven pieces of wood, twigs really, in her hand. She said,

"Umm Murad wants you to take these with you. When you go to your home make sure to burn one of the pieces of rolled paper and a twig at the Morning Prayer calls. Once you do that, collect the ash and dissolve it in a glass of water and drink it. You should repeat this ritual for the next seven days and you will be safe from then on."

I shook my head, affirming her request, and said nothing. Lulu grabbed the rolled papers and twigs and I was going to grab

132

the beads, but that girl was faster than me. She slammed her hand on top of the beads and promptly shoved them in her pocket with the piece of cloth.

I was going to ask her how much I owe her, but Lulu was quicker than me; she can be witty and fast to react at times. She said,

"Pay her 25,000 dinars."
I dropped a 25,000 dinar bill on the mattress in front of me and thanked her. Once we were out, we took a dash through the allies in search of rational daylight and flagged down the first taxicab out of the dungeons.
    "How did she know about all these things?"
    "That's why they call her a fortune teller." Lulu exclaimed.
    Then she immediately said,
    "She knows what she is doing."
    "I came because I had an incident in my house. Now I am wondering what else is waiting for me there." I kept wondering what was in those rolled papers. I wanted to take a look at what was written in them, but Lulu would not give them to me. We almost had a brawl but I knew I would lose with her. I did not know whether to laugh or take the whole matter even more seriously. It just added more mystery and unanswered questions to my predicament. Lulu said,
    "You are going to follow the instructions, right?" She had a smirking look on her face.
    "I said yeah, sure, why don't you try it first and see how it works. This trip raised more questions than it answered. In some ways, she had a general sense why we were there. I hope you didn't do some explanations to her before we went there."

"How could you say that?"

"Just wanted to set the record straight, you have not contacted her in any shape or form before we went there."

"No, I did not" then I asked the lady, and she said, she did not know we were going there until this morning when both of us came over." I was satisfied with their answers, they sounded sincere.

At home I was ready for another Turkish coffee without the traditional fortune telling, I had had more than my share for one day. I knew what Lulu was going to do once we get home, and I caught her doing just that in the kitchen. She was opening those rolled papers and reading the inscriptions in them. I quickly said,

"You are upsetting the Jinns and they will not take it lightly." She gave me a grim look, and kept doing it anyway. But while she was doing that, Mimi was barking her head off and going around in circles, twirling endlessly. I was flabbergasted to see that lovely dog in such a pandemonium. Lulu was screaming,

"Mimi...Mimi" while clenching the twigs in her right hand. When she opened her hand, her palm was completely turned to purple. I said,

"You see, I told you." When the dog calmed down she went hiding under the table in the corner, and Lulu dropped the twigs on the floor and backed away from them as if it was the devil. She completely froze and had both hands open. She had a horrified look on her face and could not utter a word. I for one looked at the ceiling and the cupboards, hoping nothing would come tumbling down on our heads. Thank God none of that happened. Nothing made sense to me, it was something

134

about keeping bad Jinns away and pleading to Allah for help, but it seemed Lulu had upset the balance of the universe, at least the universe in that kitchen, and the Jinns took it out on poor Mimi and Lulu too. I led Lulu to the nearest chair and brought her a glass of water. Her sisters came in and wanted to know what happened. Once they heard about the fortune teller story. Janan said,

"You need to rub your hands in virgin olive oil and garlic."
Lulu would do anything to make it go away now.
"I will do that right now."
"You have to do it for seven days to undo the curse of this fortune teller Umm Murad and her Jinns." I did not know whether to laugh or take it seriously. It seemed that the girls were dead serious about the remedy and so was Lulu after her encounter with the forces of Jinns. I told her that,
"I will get you extra virgin oil to get the double effect, and make sure it will go away in seven days like Janan said." I said that while I was giggling loudly. She was in no mood for a joke, though. I should not have been swayed by Lulu's words – I should have stayed home; now she had had a brush with the Jinns and their wrath at her disrespectful deed.

I felt that the whole new escapade with the fortune teller and Lulu made things worse than before. All were signs in a way of forces playing beyond explanations. I had the feeling a major event was about to happen in the house, my new house, and I had no choice but to be part of it. Somehow I felt Nejim held the key to the mystery, as he was there through it all, and he might have some explaining to do, one way or the other. Maybe I was wrong about him but so far no harm had been

135

done except Lulu's purple right hand, and I wanted to keep it that way. She could live with a purple hand for a while but that was enough for all of us. Either way I had not noticed any entrepreneurial desire on his part (and I saw it with most people these days) so there had to be something else binding him to me and this strange situation, something deep and not easy for him to talk about. The atmosphere here made most Iraqis into self proclaimed businessmen whether they had an evil intention or a pure profit motive on their minds; greed is universal after all, and not fussy about the company it keeps. In that sense Nejim came over as an honest person, although there was obviously some unfulfilled business he had on mind which I hoped I was not part of. My experiences with him so far just added to the intrigue of my stay in this benighted country of ours, something that I would remember for many years.

I felt I ought to ask him something, to see what he was hiding from me. But how could he know anything about this mysterious business, and why? I would have to confront him sooner than later, or I would spend the rest of time here in sleepless nights. I had the certain feeling that somehow he was one – or two – steps ahead of me, an eerie feeling that was going to keep me on my toes as long as I was going to be in that house, waiting and waiting for the unknown. I promised myself that I would get to the bottom of it by the next day. I needed to find out, and stop my endless wondering; obviously the answers were not available to me in my own modest way of thinking.

I spent most of the day with the girls. Every once in a while one of us got up and asked Lulu if we could take a look at her hand, but that was no laughing matter to her. I was sure it would be alright by the next day. Curiously, I now felt like I had had a lot of fun today. I needed to go back to the house and feed the bird, and look at that hole or what's left of it, before it got dark. Maybe by now the whole house had been swallowed by oblivion and I would be free again. As I approached the house, everything seemed normal from a distance. The front of the house looked dry, as if nothing had happened. Even the garden looked like it needed watering. Abu Sabah was there; I went to talk to him and see if he had noticed any unusual thing around the garden. The first thing he said when he saw me,

"The garden needs water."
"Yes, it looks dry to me, not much water." I was going to say, "You should've seen it yesterday." But I didn't. Instead I tested him a little.
"The Jujube tree in the back, it may need a little trimming."
"I wouldn't touch that tree. It looks good to me anyway." He said that in such an emphatic why that it made me wonder. The gardeners around here had their own way of knowing what was good and what wasn't, and it seemed that the Jujube tree was on Abu Sabah's bad list. I was going to tell him to stay away from that evil spot near the gate, but I didn't have to; he seemed to already know that there was a problem somewhere there. I noticed he was always avoiding that area and left it almost untouched. I was going to ask why but changed my mind; with Abu Sabah, I didn't think I would get a straight answer anyway.

Sabr was in a jubilant mood when he saw me coming in. The cucumber and watermelon I left him had withered in the heat like fried onions in a saucepan. I made a feast for him, a combination platter of fresh cucumber, grapes, date, and white cheese, and refilled his water tub. He was thankful and expressed that with his usual array of tunes after he got a good fill. I was always thrilled when he did that kind of display of gratitude and he certainly knew how to cheer me up, no matter how bad the day was. I felt better that evening and had a good night's sleep for a change, not worried about tomorrow and the house and the host of problems that came with it. There is an old Iraqi saying that seems apply at a moment like this, "Once you reach the end of the rope make a big knot and let it be". I felt like I was about to get there. I was reaching the end of my rope here; all these problems that came with the house were not part of the deal. I thought it would be free sailing but so far it hadn't been anything of the sort.

Chapter 10

The Spell

That afternoon, I left a message for Nejim in his shop to come over. It was some time in the evening when he showed up. I felt it was time for me to have a serious talk with him, a man-to-man sort of talk. I prepared a big pot of tea and laid out some local sweets. I wanted to know what was behind all these unusual things happening here in this house and I wanted to know how serious it was. I knew this much: Nejim was part of it one way or the other. He showed great fascination with the house and the garden itself from the first day he set foot in here. He had given me hints in the past but I never got to the bottom of it, partly because I felt it wasn't serious enough to let it out in the open. I was waiting for him to bring up the subject. When he left yesterday without saying a word right after the water went back in the hole, he was pleased somehow or perhaps worried, I couldn't tell either way, but I wanted to know why. I had the feeling he knew something I did not know; perhaps he was an intricate part of it all. But I did not want to ask him earlier. The thought had occurred to me many times, but somehow I felt the time was not right. I had never believed in any superstitious and supernatural powers in my life. These things did not happen and did not exist, and if someone were to tell me about it, I would consider it a big practical joke. I believed that any mysterious event must have a logical scientific explanation

140

behind it. But now I had my own doubts. I saw what happened here in front of my eyes. I knew Nejim was probably a believer in the supernatural, and would not have much sympathy for my need for logical explanations. Regardless of all that I was driven to find out something today; I felt I was about to hear a strange story from him. Needless to say I wanted some assurance that these things would not get out of hand, so I said,

"I didn't see you yesterday, you left immediately right after the water disappeared back in the hole."

"Yes, I had to leave to the slaughterhouse to get meat for my shop. I didn't mean to leave right away and leave you alone without talking to you."

"Its time for you and me to have a little talk." He looked me in the eyes and clutched the tea cup in his hand firmly, and nodded his head, affirming the feeling I had. He spoke quite softly, almost inaudibly, and said,

"I know, you want to know, I can see you are uncomfortable with what's going on here in this house, and I don't blame you."

"I noticed many extraordinary things that are going on when you are around and when I am alone too. Some of the things are related to water more or less, but when I saw the water in that hole just get swallowed back in, in a matter of minutes, for me or anyone else with a sensible view of life that was unacceptable. To tell you the truth I was baffled, and who wouldn't be? It was beyond any reasonable explanation that I can think of. I know about water and soil. I make a living designing things around water and soil and I know there is no such thing in the real world. It was like magic happening here in front of my eyes. I know you showed great interest in

141

the house and the garden from the minute you were here, for reasons you have not explained. I am sure that you may have a perfectly good explanation for everything that has happened, and I would like to hear it from you."

"I know how you feel; of course you have a right to know. I think it's time for you to know the real story, not only because you are part of it but also because of your safety."

"Well we pushed the envelope a bit here, and I want to know why I am part of it."

"What I am about to tell you has been a deeply guarded secret in my family over the years, and it has been passed on from one generation to the other for as long as we can remember. Not many people know about what I am about to tell you, unless they are intimately connected to this secret, but now it's the time for me to tell you, because you are part of it too since you opened the door of this house after all these years."

"How I am part of anything I do not know about?"

"Please listen to me Abu Wa'el and hold back your judgment until later on. I have the feeling that you don't believe in these things, but Allah can do many things that do not make sense to us – it's perfectly normal for Him. Sometimes we have to resign to the will of the unknown and accept it in our lives. "

I felt the deep sense of purpose in his voice. My thoughts were that I was about to hear a confession, perhaps a secret, and it had better be a good explanation that made sense to me. So I nodded my head and said,

"Please carry on." He went on resolutely saying,

"This land is as old as the human race on this earth. History was written here, and no doubt it will be for a long time to come. Long time ago there was a caravan route led from a very far land through the treacherous mountain passes of Persia into Baghdad. The east route to Persia went right through this area to Baghdad and then continued to other lands. Traders and raiders took this arduous route but mostly ordinary people trekked along peacefully for one reason or another.

In the old days there used to be travel inns, called "Khan" – sort of travel lodges along that caravan trail. These travel lodges were scattered all along the trail but mostly they were located near a source of water, and they were spaced a day's ride apart more or less. It's a place for people and animals to take a break from their long journey, to rest and wash up before they continue their ride again to their destinations. Here, these travel lodges were normally built around wells, to supply the passengers and their animals with water. I believe on this spot where we stand right now there was one of these caravan inns and one of these water wells. This was the last stop for people before reaching Baghdad. The trail from here on split; one went east-west and the other one went north, deep in the mountains. The secret is in the well itself. It holds a dark history. Something happened here that stayed with us until this moment. I grieve about it every day and it's in the back of my mind at all times."

"What kind of dark history can a well hold?" I asked, and he continued his story,

"On one hot summer day, like today but a long time ago, a divine master was passing through with his family and entourage. It was his last stop before reaching Baghdad. He was on the last leg of his journey to meet his people in Baghdad. They were awaiting him desperately as he was the last of his divine lineage and defender of their cause. Among his own, he had a small child. The child was four years old, the only son of his father, and the last family heir." Nejim paused for a moment, distraught and almost with tears in his eyes. Then he muttered,

"Fate took a dark turn that day not only for that child but for everyone around him, a turn that we remember to this day. At some point, the child wandered away on his own, leaving his mother and the guards. He innocently climbed up the ledge of the well in the yard – nobody knows why until this day, and somehow fell into the well. When people heard his cry they rushed out to the well, only to find him deep in the water. They could hear the child crying for his mother but could not see him. His shadowy image appeared to the eyes and disappeared in the dark, gulped by the waves of the water. Many of the men tried to rescue him. One after the other climbed down the well but could not reach him. Once they touched the water they disappeared themselves too; the child kept going on deeper and deeper, crying for help till his voice fainted away as if there was no bottom to the well. The boy and the men never came out. His parents and everyone around them were stunned in disbelieve. Twelve men in all vanished in the depths of the well like nothing had happened that day. The well swallowed them all. Immediately after what happened, the well dried out, but there was no bottom to the well, not that anyone could see, and no trace of those who vanished that day." Nejim paused for a moment; he was visibly shaken and his body was trembling. Then he kept going to say,

"The parents of the boy waited and waited by the well side for days, praying to Allah for the safe return of their child back to them, with no avail. His mother's weeping voice echoed in the dry well and came back to her with no answer from her beloved son. The father was torn from reality and dazed. Finally, heartbroken, they resigned to the will of Allah and accepted their fate. It was written, the father said. The story says he kept wondering for the rest of his life saying, It was written – It was written –" Then Nejim paused and took a long sip out of his cup of tea, and looked at me try to catch any reaction from me. I was amazed by the story and felt for him. But I had the feeling there was more to his story. When he finished his tea, he said,

"The owner of the caravan inn was very grieved and felt he was responsible for the disappearing of the divine master's son. He sat in a dark room for days praying and pleading to Allah for help, and one day a pair of bulbul birds appeared in the small window where he was sitting, then followed by more. We do not know what happened that day for him. But he broke from his reclusive room and came out. He vowed to close his lodge for good and move on to the mountains seeking redemption for his soul. He tore down the lodge building brick by brick, and filled the well with stones the best he could and sealed it for good. When he had finished, he casted a thousand year spell on the well. He said no one will ever reopen the well again for another one thousand years, and said in that thousandth year the spell would be over. There will be a stranger coming from a very far away land – but yet he is one of our own, he will free the souls of the missing child and those twelve men with him who went after him. There will be water and joy on this day and those who vanished in the well will come out as birds flying in the sky, filled with delight at their new freedom; there will be other signs too – signs only a few people would know how to read. After we see those sign the spell will be broken." Then Nejim said,

"It has been one thousand years since that incident happened."

I gasped and almost fell off my chair when I heard the last part of this unreal tale. I have to admit, it was a powerful story that sent a shiver down my spine. Was I supposed to believe in this bizarre tale? As a history buff of Iraq myself, I had never heard of such strange story before, a child disappearing into a well along with his guards. I had read about Ali Baba and Sinbad, but nothing about a boy fallen in a well! I did not want to give any negative reaction. But clearly I was taken by the event of this tale; how much truth there was in it, I did not know. I knew simple people have the tendency to exaggerate old tales in this part of the world. But although Nejim looked simple he was far from it; he had an advance degree in agriculture from the University of Baghdad and he would not tell that kind of story unless he intimately believed in it.

"That is a truly breathtaking revelation; I am profoundly touched by your story Nejim." I said to him. But he wanted to hear more than that from me. He wanted to hear, "I believe every word you uttered today and I am with you all the way." I could not say anything to ease up his feelings. In fact I wasn't sure if any of the things he said were for real, it just has to be a story passed on from one generation to the next. Then he said,

"The signs are all around us now, and I feel the time has come."

"You want to tell me that it has been one thousand years since the boy disappeared?"

"Yes, and the well is right here in this house."

"And that hole is the well?"

"That's possible, I am not sure where it is at right now. It is somewhere around here."

"There is no well here. My sister lived here for over thirty years; there was no well here before or now."

"The well was sealed until now."

"Are you telling me that all that water is coming from that well?"

"Maybe, but It's not only that Abu Wa'el; it's you who will free this boy."

"Me! Why me?"

"I have been waiting for so long, for the right person. I knew he was coming this year, this summer, but I did not know who he was. I waited for a sign. On that day when you first saw me on your doorsteps, I was sitting in my house, and all of a sudden water started seeping out of my chair. I knew I better rush to the house. When I got here I saw your car parking outside. Your name popped up on my lips the minute I saw you, for some reason I cannot explain"

"I am a person who does not believe in supernatural things. Everything has an explanation behind it, a logical explanation that a rational human being would understand; at this moment you are giving me an irrational explanation."

147

"You asked me before how did I know your name when I first saw you?

"Yes, how?"

"Believe me Abu Wa'el, that's the name I heard in my head before I knew you. There will be other signs – some are pleasant some are not, but when it comes to your safety you are my first priority and not me. I will do anything to protect you, and you can count on that."

"I thank you for your dedication to your cause and to my safety. I hope there will be no need to test either one."

"I am here to fulfill my destiny, as all of us are, including you, and my destiny is to protect you. There are evil powers in play too and we have to be watchful of our surroundings at all times. Evil will make one last stand to forbid the natural conclusion of the spell. You are an intricate part of this conclusion. I may do some things that may not make sense to you, but in the long run things have their own purpose. But Allah the most merciful will protect all of us from evil deeds. I have to do my job and as for the rest, Allah will take care of it. Sometime in the future when you go back to your home, you will be tested again, but God will be beside you and shield you from all harms, you can mark my words on that. We are all following a destiny that has already been written."

"You have really stunned me now, and I have no more words to say to you."

"I know, and I am terribly sorry for putting you in such a situation, but I need your help. Everything will be revealed to you very soon."

I kept listening to him with a look of disbelief on my face. My jaw almost dropped to the floor.

"Everything will be revealed to me in tea leaves." I thought joking to myself.

Nejim seemed unflustered by my reaction, he was expecting that response, but he did not care much whether I believed him or not. He was assured down in his mind that I would be with him all the way as "It was written." He was a man on a mission, on a destiny of his own to fulfill. I wondered where he fit in this entire grand scheme, a man of considerable faith, like most of the Iraqis. Unforeseen events have a little if any room in the lives of the people here. But Iraq, Mesopotamia, is different than the rest of the Middle East, and the Arab world. It has always been a land of a mystical glory and divine spirituality for thousands of years.

I decided that moment that I would go on doing what I was planning to do, repair the house and live in it while I was here, and if more of these mysterious nonsensical incidents happened to me, I would brush them aside and wouldn't let them distract me or scare me off – at least as long as my safety wasn't compromised. But I wanted to know who Nejim was, and why he was driven to fulfill his destiny, as he put it. I wanted to be careful. I did not want to hurt his feelings or insult him in any way. I asked him again,

"I do not understand where you fit in this story." he gave me this humble look and said again,

"I am a descended of the lodge keeper. Father to son we were entrusted with this secret throughout the generations.

We had to stand guard on this land and would not let anyone disturb the earth more than it should be, waiting for the day after one thousand years to come and set free those who vanished that day. But keep in mind, you are the key to unraveling this event, and you must be safe at all costs, even if I have to sacrifice my life for you. Remember; if I go away, God forbid, my son Karrar will take over my place. He is still young but very well aware of his destiny too, and he will do anything to keep you safe." Now you've got me worried, I thought to myself. Am I in danger here? And what kind of danger is it? I have fixed the house and made extra effort to repair the window bars and the front door. Maybe I better rethink the security situation again, and what kind of danger could befall me. So I told him,

"I don't know what to do now, Nejim."
"I am sorry about that Abu Wa'el, but it would be prudent for you to be very careful. If anything happens, I am just around the corner. I have a mobile phone now, I just bought one yesterday; call me the minute you need my help, do not hesitate."
"Is there anything else I need to know or do to make this house safer?"
"As a matter of fact, yes there is. I was thinking about that the other day. I would suggest fortifying the backyard door with a few more iron bars, put two more iron latches on each terrace door upstairs, and on the front garden gate. I will bring you a heavy duty chain and lock that will be visible from the outside. Also, I will put a floodlight right outside in the direction of the garden. This light will stay on at all times, that way everything will be clear to you before you enter the house when you come at night and also when you wake up in the

middle of the night. I will get you a supersize flashlight; you keep it handy for when there is no power."

"I agree with you; can you make arrangement again for the welder to come back here tomorrow, so we can finish the work and have a peace of mind?"

"I will."

That night I was up till dawn thinking about what Nejim had got me into. I watched TV till around twelve o'clock when the power went out, and the house went into gloomy silence, a trumpet of silence, swimming in endless darkness. I put Sabr in the front kitchen window, as if he was my guard dog, as in a sense he was. This bird recognized strangers immediately and would start twitching and rambling, making a wonder of noises which mostly had alarming tone to them. I am by nature a very light sleeper. I walked to my room and closed the door, but I could hear him in my dreams from my bedroom. When he did that kind of thing, I had learned there was a reason for his wary sounds. I quickly rushed to the kitchen to see that weird cat eyeballing him in the dark, and he was not a happy bird then. I contemplated putting a piece of cloth on top of the cage to silence him, but I thought that would defeat the purpose of his presence, since he was trying to prove his usefulness and be up to the job he was seeking. He was trying hard to fulfill his share of the bargain although I was perfectly content with his beautiful birdsongs in the morning and eloquent display of gratitude every time he saw me around, a royal greeting from a bird that had been trapped in time.

I woke up in what seemed like the middle of the night at the sound of the Morning Prayer call, and gazed through the kitchen window. Apart from the Muezzin call to pray, there was a deafening silence all around the neighborhood. In a sense it was still a peaceful and tranquil dark night. I was happy for a moment. The lust of life in this house awakened my senses, and rejuvenated my quest for more, although I had to be on constant alert; any unusual sound alarmed me and made a bit edgy. I wondered what the new day would bring to me. I thought about what Nejim had told me and I began to believe him. In many ways he was right. I thought about that fortune teller and her magic concoction; maybe things really were like they seemed to be and just like he said. I thought about the signs and the spell; not one thought escaped my mind and I linked it in my mind and cross-referenced it as if I were setting out spreadsheets in real life. Each element had its mysterious place in the sequence: as it was, is and will be – the hidden future. I was tired again and had no desire to unravel anymore of the charade of nonsense no matter how much truth was in it. When all ended, it would be the same as it was for all these years, tucked away in a history only a few knew and understood.

When I fell asleep again, I dreamt of cloud moving in the sky, a restless kind of day that rarely happened in Iraq. I was a young man then and we were heading home in my dad's car, almost at the end of our street, but we slowed down and suddenly the cloud turned to a thunderstorm and started raining hard. For some reason it impelled me to roll down the side window and I looked out of the car up into the sky. The cloud cleared a bit and there it was a human palm print in the sky. No one could see it except me. It was the left-hand palm and I was sitting on the left side of the car in the backseat, I don't know why. The palm was so vivid to my eyes that I could clearly see every single line in it, even the ones in each finger. I could see the life line, the head line, but the clearest one was the fate line. I felt the hand was not mine, but I did not know who it belonged to! Then the hand started to grow in size; it was getting bigger and bigger until engulfed the sky and turned everything around us to complete darkness. I woke up sweating in terror and could not breathe properly. I wondered what it was all about. Was it one of these signs Nejim was talking about? And what was the meaning of that sign? It was a nightmare. I decided not to share the dream with anyone, not before I knew the meaning of the dream myself – even Lulu would not know about this dream. I felt that moment that there was something inside, something from the past wanted to come out, a dark moment I had years ago.

I kept thinking about what Nejim had said about my safety. I had a deadly arsenal here in the house. I had a Browning 9 mm handgun, a favorite for Iraqis (they call it number thirteen as it takes thirteen rounds) and another one in the chamber, a 380 Star which was called short 9 mm here, and a score of AK 47 rifles; I kept one behind each door that led to the outside. I was ready for every eventuality no matter how terrible the omens might be. I was ready and I would not let anyone into my property no matter what. In my mind I had two parameters to defend; the first one was along the road and the backyard fences, and the second one was the formidable living quarters inside the house. The doors to the outside had double doors, an iron bar gate and then the wooden one, and the window bays were covered by iron bars too. This was my fortress. An attempted breach of my secure perimeter would face intense firepower, regardless of the consequences. I also developed a procedure on how to leave and enter the house. I was sure that these are essentials and every Iraqi had one in advance to protect his property and family in such a lawless country.

The morning came in as slow as it could be. I woke up half asleep, made myself a cup of tea and a couple of boiled eggs. I did not want to see anybody, not for now anyway. I put a chair outside in the front verandah and Sabr came along outside with me, trailed by his companion, the earless cat. I hung up his birdcage way up out of the reach of this cat. I wasn't sure if she was jealous or contemplating an evil act on this poor fellow, either way it did not look good. I hoped that the cat would recognize the bird as a part of this household and quit harassing him, at least if she wanted to be part of the happy family here too. She was a well-treated cat and getting a good share of the top meat cuts that Nejim was supplying me with. Sabr, I and the little cat spoke comfortably in the cool air of the morning before setting out on our exciting day. I was eating fresh top filet mignon cuts, courtesy of Nejim's butchery shop. Here all beef cuts were priced the same regardless of where the meat cut came from, but my first option was none other than filet mignon. I listened to the radio for a while as I fed both critters, the bird and the cat, and I walked back inside to watch the TV news, after I told the cat to behave herself and leave the bird alone. I kept reminding her to act in a civilized manner when she was among us. Some cats keep staring at a bird in his cage till he drops dead of terror. I certainly didn't want that to happen to this young fellow, Sabr. He was too nice to be wasted in such way.

The hot sun had an early start today. I got the bird inside and closed the door, when suddenly I heard someone knocking on the driveway gate. It was Nejim. There was an old Russian truck parked in front of the house, with a big industrial engine in the back bed and electric cables wrapped around one side of the truck. It was a welding machine that Nejim had brought in to work on the doors and windows. The welder brought in half a dozen door latches to put on the outside doors and the roof top terrace doors upstairs, and half-inch steel bars to fortify the windows and metal doors. They unloaded their equipment and the steel bars. Nejim gave the man a tour around the house showing him the upgrades we needed. He designed the steel bars to fit on the first floor windows no more than three inches apart, and welded them securely to the windows. Each outside door had and extra double door latch secured firmly from the inside. He started his old machine and it huffed and chuffed for a couple of tries then cranked up with a loud noise, while a mist of diesel fuel spat out over our heads. By the end of the day, I thought I had made a fortress out of this house – plus I had my broody singing bird Sabr and other lethal means, so I might have secured living quarters for a while here. Nejim shared my relief and showed a great sense of accomplishment. We looked like we were getting ready for a big battle coming soon. It was just the sense I had lately. The only time I felt vulnerable was when I entered the house. I had to stop the car and get out, then open the gate and drive the car inside. At night when there was no electricity, the floodlight I had installed was out and the entire house, garden and driveway were shrouded by darkness. I had to leave the car light on until I open the front door, with one hand always on my handgun, and then I had to double back to turn off the car light, lock the car, and flip the electricity switch up for the generator. It was during those few minutes that I felt unsafe and vulnerable. Anybody could be waiting for me hiding in the garden, but once I was inside my fortress I felt secure and relaxed.

Chapter 11

Ghosts of the Past

A few weeks had passed and I was almost feeling at home in my house. My life was a lot easier now. All the basics were running, electricity, water and such, except the phone line. The old phone was sitting in the hallway, waiting for some stimulation after all these years, but the line was dead. I asked Nejim about the phone line, and he said,

"Every time the government string up the phone lines, thieves cut them down and sell the cable lines. Finally, the lines went underground in trenches, but that did not deter the thieves either, they dug them out and stole the phone cable lines again." I said,
"Why don't the government, police or someone do something about it." There was a feverish feeling for thievery among those who were down and out. Before the invasion there was the heavy-handed government to keep things in order, but now there was no law and order in the streets and it was a case of anything goes.
"I guess it's going to be a while before things get back to normal."
"I wouldn't be surprised if those who strung up the phone lines in the morning are the same people who yanked it out at night." I was perplexed when I heard that. It was true almost everywhere, and it was going to stay that way for a

157

while until people realized that by doing so they were hurting themselves in the long run.

Nejim told me that there was an internet cafe on the main Palestine Road. I went there. There must have been over twenty-five desktop computers packed into a small space. In the evening there was a long waiting line. During Saddam's era the internet was forbidden, but it was relaxed a bit in 2002 and e-mail exchanges were allowed for a few privileged people. The Spider Café (that's what it was called) stayed open till late at night; I tried to avoid going there when it was crowded because the café could be one of these prime targets for suicide bombers going around looking for a target.

The long nights in this house exhumed many bad memories of the past that I thought I had buried when I left Iraq some thirty years ago. I felt that the bad dream I had weeks ago was part of what happened to me when I was a young man then, but I still couldn't explain the clear lines in the palm and what it meant. I spoke to no-one about my feelings, but now I saw it coming back to me in this house, more often than my conscious mind was comfortable with. I sort of tucked it away in my memory, way in the back and deep, so I would not reach down to it. It was painful. The only times that I would allow these memories to re-emerge was when I was among my family, and I only saw them once in every so many years. We would exchange glances when the subject unintentionally veered to that day in the hot summer of 1973. We would stop and nod our heads, then manage to change the subject again. It was painful to all of us. We spared the agony of details to some other time that never came, and left the younger generation wondering what it was all about. My Mom never spoke about it for the rest of her life, as if her sister and niece never existed, but I am sure they were there with her until the day she left. She was there on that day with me; her knees knocked and gave way below her, leaving her collapsed on the ground at the first glimpse of her sister memories. She went through a state of convulsion, screaming at the top of her lungs and weeping, typical of our past. My father did the same, though he never mentioned it and never questioned why, as if it was the will of God, and we never questioned his wisdom. God bless their souls.

But lately since I came back to Baghdad and now in this house, I had been visited by these images, the ghosts from the past come to awaken me, in my dreams, in my days, and in my nights and I did not know what to make of it. Despite my enormous capacity for blocking these awful memories and others, this particular one strangely became more frequent, somehow it opened the door for me to peek in, and to taste the past, looking back at that horrible day in the year of 1973, and looking at those images of the past. To my great amazement, I found out that they are still glued to my memory with all the crisp details, smells, and feelings, all smothered in the heat of that summer day in Baghdad. The anniversary of that date was rapidly approaching, and I was powerless, I had no choice but to let it out, and talk about it in my dreams; perhaps I could ease the pain and let those ghosts of the past rest back again in my deep unconscious for good, but I did not want to and I would hide them deep again.

It was around 4:30 in the afternoon of that hot summer day, and my mother wanted to visit my sister on the other side of town, I volunteered as usual to give her a ride. We lived in

Dawoodi District and my sister lived in the Arassat area. In those days there were no highways; the usual route was to navigate through side roads until reaching the southern entrance of the Republican Palace then, turning east across the river, and take the only bridge to the other side of Baghdad.

A few days earlier, there was a major coup in the country against the Baath regime and the rising star Saddam Hussein. The Baath party was going through a ground-shaking power struggle. Saddam was on the move, eliminating all possible rivals among the old and strong party members. The Chief of Security and Intelligence Nahdim Ghzar was a powerhouse of his own. His name rattled all Iraqis when it was mentioned; we were fearful of his name even in our own private quarters. An imminent clash was about to happen between these two ruthless killers, who stopped at nothing to achieve their goals. For Saddam, Ghzar was the ultimate nemesis, an obstacle in the way of securing his grip on power in the country. He ruthlessly consolidated his control on the government – all except for the security organization, which was in the hands of his archenemy Ghzar. Early that year Saddam started his own security apparatus, attached to the presidential palace, and began interfering with Ghzar and his operations.

The radio announcer came blaring about a coup attempt on the beloved President and his Deputy Prime Minister Saddam Hussein. The head conspirator was the Chief of Security and Intelligence Nahdim Ghzar. But the coup had failed, the radio proclaimed, and Ghzar was on the run, heading towards the Iranian border. Soon the news came that he had been caught and executed. Saddam went into his first round of eliminating the suspicious party members who he disliked. The following weeks and months, Baghdad was in a state of terror, a string of random killing of innocent people with horrifying ruthlessness stunned the people of Baghdad. It became known as the time of the Abu Tubar incidents, the Hatchet Man.

On that afternoon my father got ready to leave for his clinic, not far away from our house. Like all dentists and doctors in those days, he went for a second round of attending his patients until dusk and come back home around 8:30 in the evening. My mother and I hopped in the car on our way to my sister's. Just before reaching the entrance of the Republican Palace, my aunt had a nice house two doors down on the main road. She was getting ready at that time to leave for England with her daughter, Michele, to join her retired husband; a PhD, and a Sorbonne graduate in economics, he had been a deputy minister of economics in the Bazaz Administration prior to the Baath coup of 1968.

As I approached their house, strangely, I saw a cousin of ours just entering the house, and a police car pulled over at the same time. In those days two police cars used to park at all times at the entrance of the Republican Palace, which was not more than about 300 yards away. My mother and I looked, and yelled to our cousin; she turned around and shouted back at us in a horrified voice; she said,

"Michele and her Mom –" I could not hear the rest, but it was enough for me to know that something ominous had happened inside. I hit the brakes and reversed the car and came to a screeching stop right at the entrance of their house. We rushed out of the car and saw two police officers trying to open the front door with a crowbar. We tried to peek inside one of the bedrooms but could not see much. We managed to open the door just enough to take a look, but something was in the way on the floor, preventing the door from being fully opened. We pushed the door hard, it was a body! It was my aunt's. By that time, several police cars had arrived. They decided to enter the house through the kitchen door in the back. After securing the house, a police officer came out saying that there was another body laying on the floor, and a live girl in the bedroom who was soaked in her own blood. I rushed into the house to see who she was, hoping that my cousin Michele was still alive. She was a few years younger than I was, a well-mannered, beautiful tall and thin girl. Yet at that moment, I did not know whether she was dead or alive ! I knew they had a fulltime young maid there too.

I entered the kitchen door, and the stench of death was everywhere. The refrigerator door was opened. On the kitchen table there were cigarette butts standing up in an unusual way and a bottle of water stained with blood. I braced myself and took a few more cautious steps into the house; I came upon the most chilling and gruesome scene a man could've ever seen. There she was laying on the floor, face up, with a big pool of dry blood under her head. Her terrified eyes were wide open, gazing at the ceiling in a horrifying last minute look of her life. Her long hair was soaked with dry blood. My aunt's body lay against the front door; she was in her nightgown, and she had a huge slit across her head. Their maid was battling to stay alive in the bedroom, soaked in her own blood too; all of them had been raped. I turned around and saw streaks of blood drops decorating the walls and going straight up to the ceiling. The stairway rail was covered with lumps of dry blood all the way to a room upstairs. The door had been struck with a couple of blows from a sharp and heavy instrument, perhaps it was an ax, and was split into two halves right down the middle. One blow seemed to have gone astray and hit the sidewall and taken a big chunk out of it. I went downstairs to witness an ugly scene; one of the officers clumsily tried to move the body of my cousin – her body moved sideways in one piece, stiff and dry as if it was a piece of wood. That scene shocked me to the core and left an indelible mark on my life. I gaped with horror. I felt a rush of nausea invade my body, all over me, and my conscious and my soul. I took a few steps backward, realizing that this was for real.

At that moment, I could not look at any more of this horrifying sight, I was rattled, and my senses were frozen. All what I saw was her terrified open eyes in my mind, drilling deep into my core. I decided to leave. I staggered to the kitchen door and had a breath of fresh air to clear the stench of death, my own perhaps; how awful it sounded in my mind when I thought about it. I looked at my hand, the left hand, the one I had opened the door with it. I felt it sizzling and shaking. I wanted to see if it was still alive, unlike my cousin's Michele. My mom and my other cousin were waiting for me outside, looking at me, trying to read the words in my face, but there were none, only a look of agony and horror. I tried to hide my face as much as I could, and mumbled a few words,

"She is dead, both of them are dead." My mother dropped on the ground. I carried her and my cousin to the car and left. They were the first innocent victims of Saddam Hussein.

In the morning I felt that I had to reconcile my feelings. I wanted to see that house again. Their house was till there right

163

in the Green Zone. I had this reluctant feeling to see the house again after all these years, but I set off on my journey just the same, I had this stubborn drive in my veins and I could not delay it anymore. I went and knocked on the door. A lady answered the door. I did not know what to say, but I told her who I was. The house was sold many years back, and the new owner knew vaguely about what happened there so many years back. She asked me if I wanted to come in and look around inside the house. That was the last thing I wanted to do. I did not want to stir the old memories again. I froze for a while and could not say a thing, and finally managed to say "No." I turned around and never looked back.

The house was located now in the heart of the new American Embassy, and was demolished for good later on. That house was cursed forever. In Iraqi mythology, the entrance to a cursed house has to be changed. The front door has to be blocked completely and a new entrance has to be built on another side of the house. I do not know where the entrance of the new US embassy is. They should have consulted me first. I hoped the curse of that house would not spill to the new US embassy too.

Nejim.......Nejim

165

Chapter 12

Talib

As usual when I was not feeling too well, I retreated to my sanctuary; seeking comfort of mind, I decided to cross the bridge away from the Green Zone and pay Lulu a visit. But I did not want to say anything, I'd done my deed. My conscience was clear, and I hoped that it would be enough for now. There was nothing else I could do. As I was thinking about the past, I forgot myself for a while. I was in the midst of a traffic jam. I had to be careful these days, as those military convoys and unruly security SUV's streamed through the narrow streets of Baghdad. The best anyone could do was to stay out of their way and keep a comfortable distance from those vehicles. On my way I ran into several of them. I was lucky enough to pull over to the side at the right time and stayed off the road. It was getting extremely dangerous to drive around Baghdad. Those private security guards in their bombastic new SUV's were extremely aggressive and they would point their guns and even fire on people for reason or no reason. Each vehicle carried a rear sign which said "Lethal Force Stay 150 Meters Away". I didn't see how anyone could stay 150 meters away in a traffic jam on one-lane streets. The new Iraqi police and army pickup truck drivers picked up similar driving habits, and they were getting even worse; they fired their weapons in the air as they drove at lightning speed. The rest was up to you and your luck that day. I arrived there just before noon time and took refuge from the searing heat outside.

As I was about to enter the house, three American security guard SUV's zoomed in, passing the house only to get stuck in the traffic. The 150-meter rule did not apply so well in a street filled with cars getting nowhere. The front SUV driver panicked and tried to go over the high concrete median to the other side of the road. As he went over the two feet high concrete barrier he got stuck. His vehicle straddled the barrier, two wheels on each side of the road He was going back and forth and tearing up the oil case beneath his vehicle; oil started leaking on the pavement and cars on both sides jammed the street, not knowing what was going on. By the time they found out, it was too late to back off and they were stuck in a potential killing zone, not only for them but for everyone around them too. The second SUV rammed the cars in front of it crushing them into each other in one pile. The car in front of that SUV was driven by an old man. He let go the steering wheel and raised his hands in the air, I was not sure if he was praying or surrendering to the inevitable. Lulu and I were looking at this drama unfolding in front of our own eyes and could not believe what we were seeing. Then three burly American guys armed to the teeth got out of their vehicle, took one end of the front winch of their vehicle and hooked it up to the almost disabled one in front of them. As they did that, bullets started flying in all directions. I did not know who was firing at what. It takes one shot to start a deadly havoc. I quickly pushed Lulu inside the house, grabbed Mimi under my arm and closed the door behind us. The ongoing gunfire lasted almost five minutes with a barrage of explosive noises and tires squealing. We kept our heads down and waited behind a thick brick wall in the living room. Mimi was the bravest; she did not utter a whimper and kept looking at me and wondering what was going on, I wished I knew.

Ten minutes had passed since we heard the sound of the battling SUV's leaving the street, but as we tried to get up on our feet we heard a sound of moaning coming from the front of the house. I carefully opened the front door and took a peek. I saw the body of a man twisting in pain laying in our driveway. Mimi was ahead of me, jumping as if she knew who he was. It was Talib. He was hit in the left side of his stomach. The bullet exited his body in the back and left another open wound. Blood was gushing out from both ends. I hoped it was a 9 mm bullet and not the notorious 5.56 mm. I know most of these security guards carry 9 mm, MP 5's. The scene of carnage outside the house was something like from a James Bond movie; smashed cars lay everywhere, ravaged by those monster SUV's. It was an unnecessary use of force prompted by panic and sheer brutality, a completely ignorant attempt to scare the locals. I tried to talk to him. I wanted to tell him he was going to be fine and I would take care of him but his eyes were rolling back in pain. Lulu shouted from in back,
"Who is it there on the ground?"
"Its Talib, Lulu, and he's been shot real bad." She came out running,
"Oh my God." She put her hand on her face and looked terrified.
"Lulu, get me a towel or something, and a bottle of water too." Lulu ran back inside the house. His chest was heaving up and down and blood was coming out of his wounds at every move. One of his friends came over and helped me put him in the back seat of my car and put the towel under his back

wound. I had to drive against the traffic to get out of that area. He was awake all through the trip to the hospital, but he was rambling with incoherent words.

The hospital was packed with freshly injured people, "It must have been from another incident" I wondered. The corridors were crowded with people; some werelaying on the floor and bleeding; we had to wait in line for the doctor but a nurse came over and hooked Talib to an IV drip to stabilize him. When the doctor showed up he quickly examined him and said that the bullet had missed his vital organs and exited safely clean through the back, but he was bleeding profusely. He stitched him back up and gave him a heavy dose of antibiotics and asked him to go home. I asked the doctor if he had any internal bleeding, he said "No" but his answer was not so convincing to me. This was the best he could do while other maimed patients of the day were waiting in line for him, all in one day's work. I carried the tiny body to my car hoping that the doctor was right in his diagnosis. The bleeding had stopped, at least from the look of it. My pants and shirt had dry blood stains all over them but I was not really concerned about myself at that moment. I washed my hands the best I could and returned back to him. I asked his friend, "Where does Talib live?" And he answered: "Sadr City."

"Where else." I thought to myself. Of all the places around here in Baghdad, it had to be Sadr City. I made it once to the entrance of this city by mistake because there was no U-turn beyond a certain point, which taught me good lesson. I had to drive deep into the city to make it back. They should have posted a sign saying "This is your last chance to turn back"
– or something like "Beyond this point you are on your own"
– , even his friend did not want to come with me. He took a

bus ride back home and I had to make that ghastly ride there all by myself. Well, here was my chance to get acquainted with Sadr City. I just hoped he would be strong enough to give me directions when we got there.

I stopped outside the hospital at one of the makeshift pharmacies to fill up his prescription and get antiseptics and wound dressing bandages. Then I set off to the dreadful Sadr City on my own. I didn't think there could be a worse time to enter that city than now. I hoped I could make it in and out in one piece. I had crossed the Great Divide once and it was by mistake. By the time I made it to the entrance of the city, Talib gave me a feeble smile and he was able to speak up and steered me through the alleys of the infamous city to his little house. It was a hot and dusty day, the sky turned red as if the gates of hell had just opened and billowed volleys of flames our way. I was not sure how I managed to pass through the checkpoints with no questions; I believe that ID card Nejim gave me somehow had some kind of special power. I was not stopped not even once. Talib navigated me through the small roads crowded by kids and junk cars. He lived in one of those houses where half-a-dozen people lived in each room. We pulled over next to one of these straight wall houses built right at the edge of the street with small windows and metal doors. As I knocked on the door, kids from all sides started gathering up and surrounding me in a perfect synchronization. They were quiet, almost speechless while they were gazing at one of their own in a not so hearty condition. Two of them ran inside the house. A howling women's cry broke the silence. The howling turned to screaming as she saw the man I was about to carry to her house. I stayed there and tried my best to comfort her but I was silent most of the time, taken aback by the scene in front of me. I could not say a word. Inside I put him on a small mattress on the floor. Then I gathered myself and explained to her what had happened and who I was. I told her, the doctor said he was going to be fine and she needed not to worry. I told her he just needed a few days of rest. I gave the grief-stricken wife the medicine and told her to make sure that he took it every four hours, and that she needed to keep the stitches clean. I tried to give her some money but she would not accept any, she said I had already done a lot to help her husband. There was nothing else for me to do, I turned around and left, just hoping to find my way out of this city.

I was weary; my eyes had witnessed a terrible scene today. I was soaked with sweat and blood, my own sweat and someone else's blood. It dawned on me again how depressing life was around here. Talib's luck almost ran out today. I pity those who make their living on the streets; they are the most vulnerable; there is no telling when things might turn unsightly and chaotic. He was a despondent soul who was at the wrong place at the wrong time. I kept thinking about the last couple of hours. It was another one of those near misses for me, but I felt like I was getting closer by the day to the big one. I counted my blessing but how many times could this kind of thing happen before I would become a real target. I wondered when I would be down on my luck like he was. The streets of Baghdad were getting extremely dangerous not only for me but for everyone. The safest thing to do was to keep off the streets and stay home and not wander in places like this one. I still had to make my way out of Sadr City, the most dangerous place in Baghdad – if not the whole world right now.

171

My eyes were getting blurry and my legs were tired. I felt I was driving aimlessly. I was entirely unprepared for today's flare-up. Of all the things that could go wrong, I certainly didn't want to be in a friendly fire or a case of mistaken identity.

"I think it's getting to me now." It seems I am going through endless streets and corners in a city of which I have no clue where it starts or ends.

"I am exhausted now." I kept jabbering to myself. I wanted to get home before my body gave up and I would be another body found on one of the side roads here. Driving through these streets rattled my nerves and the heat and smell of blood in the car did not help at all. Some people looked at me as if I was from another planet; others did not bother at all, but thanks to my little car that made me blend in and disguised my true identity. I am sure many thought that I was another taxicab driver heading for work on the other side of town; I did not mind. I had a little bubble compass under my back view mirror. I kept my eyes on it every time I made a turn; I knew I needed to go west once I found my way to the main road. Finally, I saw the dip in the highway separating the ugly and not so ugly parts of town, the Great Divide, ah – I let out a great sigh. I just needed to find the overpass bridge and cross the Great Divide to the other side. I knew where I was heading. I yelled,

"Home."

Chapter 13

The Black Hand Man

I knew I had my own foolishness here to contend with. My life in this house was getting ratcheted up by these unreal events, and for a few moments I thought Nejim was the source of all the aggravations that had hit me. Nejim's obsession with his fable took another peculiar twist one night when I invited him to come over. I was unaware of him when he opened the gate and entered the house; perhaps he did that deliberately so I would not notice his presence. But accidently I caught a glimpse of him at the end of the garden staring at the grass again. I wondered what he was doing now, and then he knelt down and suddenly started taking handfuls of dirt and grass, throwing it at his face, almost smothering his body with it too. I was stunned and could not make sense of this uncanny behavior. I dropped everything I had in my hand in the kitchen sink and darted out towards him. As I got closer I could swear I saw that patch of grass in front of him glowing in the dark for a moment. I took a couple of steps back as I was rethinking what I should be doing next. I thought I better not get near him or anywhere near that corner of the garden. I kept my distance and went back inside the house, before I took a second look at this odd event taking place in front of my eyes. I was absolutely amazed at the things happening here in this garden, everyday there was something new and bizarre. Terrified or amazed at his behavior, I could not tell. Finally my patience

174

ran low, I opened the door and rushed out there and asked him in a stern voice,

"Can I ask you what are you doing?" I caught him off guard but that did not deter him and he went about doing the same thing as if he was in the midst of a sacred ritual, more like an ecstasy, but he wasn't. He tried to lever himself up in slow motion. I grabbed him by his arm and helped him up, then he leapt to his feet; but still he could not take his eyes from the grass in front of him, then he went on saying,

"I just want to check on that hole again."

"There is no hole there Nejim."

"I want to make sure of that." He must have lost his mind, or had instant insanity just struck him in this dark night? I thought to myself. I held him up on his feet and jerked him a bit, hoping he would come back to his senses. I was genuinely saddened by this affair. I could see the depth of his affection to his cause, but it was going too far. To me there was a line and he had crossed that line.

"Would you come inside and clean yourself up, while I make some tea." He was so confused. He nodded his head and kept rambling again with incoherent words. It seemed he had lost it for a while. I couldn't believe I would see him in such a preposterous state. I walked him to the house to clean up. I waited for him to come out and have a cup of tea. He looked better when he came out of the bathroom, and more composed. He sat for a while but was still unfocused and confused.

"I am going to call your son to come and fetch you; you don't look so well to me." He wasn't so please with that notion,

"I feel better now."

"You don't look well to me."

"I just need some rest; it's been a long day for me."

"Well let me walk home with you then." I walked home with him that night. I did not want him to wander on his own in the streets, although his home was just a couple of hundred yards away. He looked really lethargic and dragged his feet. I had just about had enough for one day; I needed some rest myself too.

Later that night, I got a startling call from him, his voice on the other end of the line was not so reassuring; he said,

"I have blisters all over my hands and arms, and its itching real bad." For a moment I thought it was poison ivy from the garden, then I thought to myself this is Iraq and not Ohio, there is no such plant in this country. Then it must be something else altogether. Whatever it was, it came from the garden; that's the only explanation I could come up with.

"I can't take you anywhere right now. I will bring you some cream to ease up the itching." It was right after midnight and the streets were under strict curfew. But I managed to walk to his house. I knocked on his door for the first time. His wife came out to the door and let me in. Nejim was laying on one side of a small room, while on the other side there were candles and Bekhoor, burning incense, and in the middle of it there was a stone half covered by a neatly displayed piece of olive green color velvet cloth embroidered with gold. He was in bed and had both his arms risen above his body. He was in obvious pain and could not move. I looked at his both hands; they looked like they had second degree burns up to his elbows and open sores too. I opened a tube of itching cream I had with me, I told his wife to apply it on the arms and hands. I took a second look at that corner where he had that big stone sitting there. I could not make sense out of it. I told Nejim that

176

I would take him to a dermatologist in the morning. Then he said in a feeble voice,

"I should not have disturbed the hole." I knew what he had in mind, and I did not want to enter in another futile discussion about that idiocy. But I said,

"Have you touched any metal thing like pieces of bombs or shrapnel there?" he said,

"No, I did not see anything, just grass."

"Something was glowing there."

"There was nothing there except grass and dirt."

"There must be something, something not visible to the eye, was it wet?"

"Not really."

"Well, listen; if it gets worse, give me a call alright, and try to get a good night's rest, we all need it."

"Yes, I thank you very much for coming over." I was thinking maybe he had come into contact with shrapnel from one of those depleted uranium munitions. But that was a far-fetched theory. Now I knew why Abu Sabah never touched that corner; maybe he had similar experience or noticed it glowing too. I left the house hoping that Nejim would get a good night's sleep. It was almost two in the morning anyway. I hugged the walls under the crescent moonlight while walking back to my house, trying to stay unnoticed, navigating through the junk cars and piles of garbage littering my pathway; it was only a couple of blocks luckily. My earless cat was leading the way ahead of me.

I had yet to sleep through a whole night in my new home. In the morning I woke up to a phone call from Lulu; it was very early. She said,

"My purple hand is not getting any better." She was getting worried sick. She said,

"Even Mimi would not let me pet her and she keeps looking at my hand." I had to calm her down first and told her,

"We need to make an appointment with a dermatologist." I had to tell her about Nejim and his own problem with his hands last night. She was rattled by the coincidence. Now I had two cases for the dermatologist. I just needed to find a good one. So I asked her, she said,

"There is one near where I live." I skipped my morning ritual of feeding my two critters and got ready to leave, while Sabr gave me an earful of singing protest.

Nejim had had a sleepless night. The itching cream I gave him seemed to have stopped the rash or whatever it is from spreading out. His wife had made an old recipe made of sticky paste. She said they tried that before and it seemed it worked, although I did not know what kind of skin rash she had treated before, but anything might help. It is made of Defla plant, Rhododendron. I always hated that plant, I've always found it a weird plant. She tried it on one arm. The dermatologists was not much of a help, he was puzzled as much as we were with the unusual color of Lulu's hand, and Nejim's illness. He thought that the purple color was no more than a stain from a rare plant, the one those twigs came from, and would fade away with time. As for Nejim's illness, he had no clear answer, but he gave him another type of itching cream fortified with cortisone. We returned back home dissatisfied, after we made a quick stop at the pharmacy. On the way back, I tried to be positive and veered off completely away from the subject. Lulu was quiet throughout the day. She had not been herself lately and she worried me some. I wanted to talk to her alone but perhaps some other time. I hate to see her withdrawn and silent like that, it just wasn't Lulu, the way she was. She'd always been vibrant and quick on her feet.

On the way back I got a call from my old good friend Emad. I mentioned to him the problem we had. He told me about a natural healer called Abu Eid el-Sawdda, the Black Hand Man. Apparently he was a well known man here in Baghdad, accredited for many unsolved illnesses. After the fiasco of the fortune teller, I was not in the mood for another magical power entering my life again; I had had my share for now. I would strictly prefer a scientific approach from now on, but that dermatologist wasn't much of a help. Emad insisted it was not like that, and would not hurt in any case. I reminded him of the fortune teller, when Lulu insisted that will do no harm and we should do it just for fun. Now, we were trying to undo some sort of a curse had stricken Lulu's hand, besides which I was not ready to visit someone I did not know in the old side of Baghdad. He said he the healer lived just across the road from Elboushja Mosque in Karada. When I talked to Lulu about that, she was upbeat on the idea. Lulu was never still, not for a moment, if she wasn't cooking she was up and down the stairs and never broke sweat, or got tired or out of breath; and that's the way she was supposed to be, not procrastinating and worried. Nejim had no comments and was willing to try anything to ease the pain. I went along on the ground that it was not my hand and my arms we were dealing with here; it was up to them to take whatever remedy this man offered them.

The Black Hand Man's store had no sign on it, but people knew who he was in that area; mention of his name brought a respectful reverent answer around the area. He was a midget, no more than four feet tall, with one arm truly black like his nickname. I wondered why he had not had a cure for his own arm. Which raised another question; how would he get rid of that purple color when he has a similar problem? I am sure Lulu felt the same way.

The store of the Black Hand Man was packed with shelves stacked up to the ceiling with all sorts of dazzling assortments of jars filled with colorful ingredients and syrups, and labeled in red and blue color ink. The old ones were covered with dust and had their labels almost peeled off, somehow giving off a more potent appearance. I wasn't sure how he managed to reach these jars given his unfortunate condition. It turned out he had an added advantage which came in a form of a long stick that had a grip-like end. I watched him sorting out his small jars as if he was fly-fishing those jars off the shelves and reeling them back to him. It was a show to behold.

The four of us stood in the front of his store that had among many things, exotic mixture of dry plants, animal skins and other wild critter parts. On the floor we noticed bones and wild animal skeletons – some were scattered around, and some were possibly of extinct animals, if not prehistoric in nature. His store was the Iraqi version of a natural medicine man, or alternative medicine store to be politically correct, but he did not care what we would call it and was obviously satisfied with his nickname and the notoriety that came with the name. I bet he had no intention of changing the color of his right arm as well, as it brought him fame and fortune.

Lulu was quick to start the conversation by saying,

"Good morning Seyedna, we have two problems we want you to take a look at."

"Good morning to you too, welcome to my store. What kind of problems you have?" he asked. I resumed the conversation by saying,

"One is the discoloring of her palm, and the other one is some sort of blisters which appeared last night after he finished working in the garden." The man could not reach to take a look at either one, so he invited us to a small room in the back of his store. We walked between the shelves, stumbling on his bone collection on the floor. Lulu opened her hand, showing him the purple color palm. His first impression was like he had seen this before. He checked out her hand, flipping it back and forth, and then he said,

"You have been to Umm Murad?" I looked at Lulu and she was looking back at me, then I said,

"Yes we have, how did you know that?"

"She is the only one who uses this type of herb."

"Is it a herb?"

"It is some sort of herb."

"What kind of herb, I hope it's not a bad one!"

"No its not, it's a special type of Hinna, dye coloring plant that react immediately with human sweat."

"I was supposed to burn it and drink the ashes afterward."

"That's possible. I do not interfere with her treatments. I normally turn back those who have been to Umm Murad, but because of my good friend Emad brought you here, I will make an exception."

"Barak Al'lah Beek, God bless you." Emad said,

"Is there a way that the stain can be removed?" I asked,

"She can use lemon juice to rub her hand ; it seems the acid reacts with the oil base that kind of plant yields. But it will take time."

"Thank God, no more garlic and olive oil." I murmured to myself. She smelled of garlic wherever she went. I just did not want her to be scared for life with this unpleasant purple stain on her hand.

"Thank you Seyedna." Lulu said with a big confident smile on her face. Then the miniature Sayedna turned to Nejim and said,

"What's wrong with his arms?"

"He was working in the garden last night; when he finished his hands started itching, and then these skin sores started to show up." He took a deep look at both arms, and said,

"I have seen these types of blisters only once in my life time before." I felt like,

"Here we go again. We are about to hear another thrilling story of magic and Jinns." But none of that happened. We were all waiting for further clarification, while the midget healer was uncomfortable and restless in his seat, but finally he broke the silence and carried on, saying,

"A man came to me some years back with similar problem but less in its severity. He acquired the problem while he was digging a trench on the other side of Baghdad. I prescribed Hudhud crushed bones, mockingbird of the Middle East, it must have something to do with birds. He was cured in seven days."

"Barak Al'lah Beek, God bless you Seyidna." Nejim replied.

"This type of treatment is very expensive. As you know, Huhud birds are almost extinct, and those who are still around are only found in the high mountains of Persia." I assured his grace that this would not be a problem. He reached up to one of those dusty jars with half-fallen labels on the top shelves using his magic stick, and brought it down with one stroke. He dusted off the jar and kept looking at it as if he was about to wake up the Jinns inside. He mumbled a few religious phrases first. But the jar would not open and seemed stuck. We backed off a bit, giving him more room – or perhaps we were not comfortable with what we were seeing. All of us kind of had the jitter these days. The stubborn jar wasn't a problem to him as he had another contraption, a self made jar opener which did the trick of opening the ancient vessel. We felt relaxed, and all of us quietly leaned forward to see the magic ingredient inside. It was pale white powder and no Jinns, thank God. He measured a couple of ounces in a prehistoric small scale, and said,

"I am going to mix it with Castor oil; you rub the infected arms twice a day, once when you wake up in the morning and the second time just before you go to bed. I guarantee you on the seventh day you will wake up cured." That wasn't so bad I thought to myself. The magic ointment came in a dark brown jar, unlabeled of course. Nejim took the jar and held it close to his heart, as if it was his life saver from a dreadful disease, which I hoped it wasn't.

Emad signaled the number five to me, at which I quickly dropped two of these red 25,000 Iraqi dinar bills on the table. The midget grabbed those two bills while whispering something to himself, then raised them to his forehead and pushed them into his small pocket. Lulu was in upbeat spirit and so was Nejim, and I hoped that this was the last of these inexplicable illness for these two guys for now.

183

Nejim.......Nejim

Like many nights in the recent past, I had another ghostly incident to contend with. Two weeks had passed, and I was feeling the anguish of guilt when I saw Lulu and Nejim somehow suffering from my deeds. Although I had nothing to do with their illness I still had a guilty feeling looming over my conscience in the dark silence of the nights. I was hoping that we were going to put behind us those unfortunate ailments with the assistance of our newly acquired help – the medicine man.

I could swear on the seventh day Nejim was completely healed, and Lulu's purple color hand was almost back to normal. She was so happy about that. She did not have to cover her hand every time someone came in and pretend it was burned while cooking. Her sisters stopped teasing her, while her dad was not sure what the problem was in the first place, as the girls never bothered explaining it to him. If he had known, he would have had the house exorcised by the priest to expel the bad spirits. Thank God it did not come down to that, otherwise it would have been the talk of the town and Lulu would've been in trouble again.

I wanted Nejim to check on those two workers who dug the hole in front of the house. I was very concerned that they may have a similar problem. I told Abu Sabah to stay away from that corner of the garden. He was ahead of me anyway; he never touched that corner – that was evident from the overgrown grass there and that weird plant too.

"Does he know something I do not know, or maybe something glowed on him like it did to me that night and kept him away?" He always amazed me with the exceptional care that he gave to the garden. But from what I had heard he did such an exceptional job wherever he worked. He was accepted by all the neighbors, if it wasn't for his mouth and gossiping. I am sure he had been spreading a few ill words about me around too; but I tried my best to be less of a subject for his unworthy gossip tales. I gave him extra money every once in awhile to keep his mouth shut – to earn his silence.

Nejim went to the Baladiya to check on these two men, but he could not find them there. He asked around to find out where they lived, but that wasn't successful either; no one knew much about them, but they knew they were always together – inseparable as if they were twins. He came back with disappointing news. It seemed both had disappeared right after they returned back to work that day. No one at work had seen them since then. Even their co-workers were wondering what happened to them. They did not even come to work to collect their monthly salaries, and when that happened, it was a sure sign something was wrong. I just hoped that they were well and had found another job somewhere else around town, or they had moved out of town, but the thought kept me worried for many days. If they were sick then they might be in real bad shape. I saw them both sinking in that mud to their shoulders. Sometimes I could not help it but to think about those poor people, I tried to help in anyway I could and give them work even when I knew they are asking twice as much or even more for a job worth considerably less; whether they were using me or not was of little important to me as long as it put more food on someone's table for another hungry child around town.

Chapter 14

The Jinns

There was something missing in Nejim's story. His story kept going round in my mind, word by word. I believed in everything he had told me about the missing child. I believed the child had been touched by God. But he had not told me everything. He had skipped an important detail. I felt there was a hole in his story, not that I thought he was lying to me. Perhaps it was unintentional. I am not sure why he did that. He might have had a purpose for doing that. There was a power struggle, or that's what it seemed to me from his account of the events of that day one thousand years ago. The mysterious disappearance of the child and twelve men with him happened because there were forces that wanted it to happen. These forces, evil forces were not dormant – they were still active until this day, or at least in his mind. And all that stuff about protecting me! Protecting me from what? His calm and almost subdued demeanor was not born of his confidence but of his fear. The man was frightened. He had been haunted by these powerful images he created in his mind. His smile sometimes puzzled me.

But I had seen the power of these inexplicable forces in action, and I had no doubt that they existed now. I had no other explanations for how that water could disappear in a flash of second back into the hole again. That needed an act of power unavailable to me or to any rational human being. It was like a black hole sucked down everything in its path. Thank God no one got hurt that day. It was nothing short of a miracle, and it seemed that miracles did happen. This was the only single act that baffled me and everything else was marginal, such as the most recent illness that struck Nejim and Lulu's hand for that matter. The fortune teller warned me of the Jinns, she mentioned that there are two kinds of Jinns, good and evil, but that was in a general sense. I am sure she says that to everyone seeking her advice. But how did she know that there was someone looking after me and protecting me from those bad Jinns and that that person held the secret to the mystery surrounding the house, and he would let me know in due time? I would just have to be patient. Even Lulu did not know that before we went to see Umm Murad, which raised the next question. How did the fortune teller, Umm Murad, know about it in the first place? Many questions and many incidents did not add up, there was something here which was beyond reasoning, was it for real? Do these supernatural powers really exist? I could happily have dismissed it all, except that water hole was still mystifying me. I was afraid even to look at it or where it was; it just gave me the shivers when I walked by it.

Nejim had left an open crack in his story; what and who are these forces? And why did they do what they did that day and keep the mystery going on till this day? Of course, I wanted to believe that none of it was true, that the mother was simply reckless and let the child wander off on his own, that he simply fell into the well, and his guards were punished for allowing it to happen. As time went by the story was modified and became a legend. But I had to go with Nejim's version of the story for now. To his family and him this was a historical event, and it was all in his hands to put a final closure to this epic saga, that had lasted one thousand years. I decided that when I saw him again, I would push him for an explanation and would not let him off the hook so easy.

I woke up in the middle of my sleep that night. I thought I heard the most beautiful voices imaginable outside the house. I quickly ran to the kitchen window to take a look at the front gate. I could swear I saw the shadows of two men right outside, but once they saw me, they quickly ran away and vanished in the dark night. Sabr was awake too and gazing at them, but he was quiet, very unusual for him. I do not know how they saw me behind the window in the dark. I rubbed my eyes and took another look, but they were gone; it was a quiet and still night. These two men were the two workers who dug the hole a couple of weeks ago, the two that I was so worried about since Nejim's illness. They were wearing the same blue working jumpsuits they had on when they were digging the hole that day, and even the dirt on their clothes was evident, as if they just had finished the job. It seemed they had not changed their clothes since then. This was getting unnerving: now I had started seeing ghosts. I did not want to go out and chase them, playing hide and seek in this dark night. I wished I could, but I had made a commitment to myself never to open the front door after eleven at night. I was confused and weary, trying to sort out the images in my mind. I double checked all doors and windows and gripped my rifle in my hands and stayed awake for the rest of the night. I kept pacing the floor nervously, looking outside every once in a while, waiting for them to come, but they were gone. I wondered how they managed to get in and get out so easily. There was a six-foot-high front fence they needed to climb over. I wished I had a

189

dog here inside the house with me; Mimi came to my mind. Although she was small, she was a good guard dog; but she was also very delicate and Lulu would not lend her to me.

In the morning I asked Nejim to check again on the fate of these two workers without telling him about my weird experience encounter the night before. He came back in the afternoon and told me that someone had spotted them, but was not sure of the details. I was going to tell him, "So did I. I spotted them too here last night." But I kept that a secret to myself for now. After last night, I had second thoughts about confronting Nejim about his story and the spell cast by his ancestor, the owner of the Khan. I thought maybe it wasn't the time to do that yet. I wanted to explore what more the fortune teller knew about the house and if she ever knew anything about the spell itself, and how she connected me to that spell. I also wanted to ask her a personal question; which is why I did not want Lulu and Nejim to be around. The question I wanted to ask was about that dream I had the other night. The dream of the left palm and what it meant. Was it related to the murder of my aunt and her daughter? This had nothing to do with the house, or Nejim – at least I hoped not; it must have deep-rooted reasons, that go back to when I was a young man. It could be related to the death of my aunt and her daughter, or it could be something else altogether. I decided to give her a visit in the morning.

I left the house, heading to Fadhel, this time on my own. I left my car at home and took a taxicab, then went on foot through the allies to that house. The same young woman opened that little window and peeked at me and saw me alone. She took a second look, she paused, then she closed the window again;

but I could hear her talking to another woman inside. I heard the other woman saying,

"I have been expecting him to come back, let him in." She opened the door and let me in. Once I was inside, I sat down in the same room waiting for Umm Murad. She immediately came in and greeted me in a more buoyant way than last time. She sought my shoulder in a kind way with her hand as she squatted in front of me. Her blind eyes were flaming red and dripping with fluid – I could not say it was tears. She said,

"I was expecting you to come back, we have unfinished business."

"Yes, Khatoon, I think we do. Last time we could not finish our session." She got her red piece of cloth out and spread it in front of me and tossed the beads on it.

"Yes that's true, what can I do for you today?"

"I am here to seek guidance. I want to ask you about what you said to me last time, about my house. What do you know about my house?" I collected the beads as usual and tossed them on the cloth seven times just as I had done before.

"All I can tell you is the same as I did last time – that your house holds a secret."

"That's what I want to know, what kind of a secret does the house hold?"

"The house is sitting on a divine place. If I were you I would not try to disturb the ground there, anyone who does that may be stricken by a bad spell. As I told you last time, things will be revealed to you in due time. I cannot tell you anymore than that for now. If nothing happen within a couple of weeks come back again and we will talk."

"Why two weeks? What's going to happen in these two weeks?"

"I can't give you any more details right now; you just have to be patient." At that moment I could not ask her for more information. I wanted to ask her how she knew about all this, but I couldn't. I was sure she would not tell me anyway and might take it as an insult. The question about my dream kept bothering me, but at the last minute I changed my mind and kept it to myself. I just felt it was hard for me to share such personal facts with another person. I thought it would be prudent to wait and maybe things would unravel in the next week or two like she said. I noticed there were no Jinns present as in last time, she skipped that ceremony altogether this time. Then she said to me,

"Did you follow my instructions? I said,

"I am ashamed to say, no I have not because we somehow had lost one of the twigs you gave us." She was not amused with that answer. I hoped she would not hit me with one of her curses; I didn't like the idea of walking around with a purple hand. I was going to tell her about the purple hand Lulu had after she tried to open those pieces of papers she gave us last time and the trouble we went through afterwards, but I was afraid that I might get on her wrong side, the bad side that is, so I kept quiet about that too. She got up and was about to leave the room when she felt I was reaching to my wallet. She said,

"La... La, No...No.", I said,

"Thank you Khatoon." And then she left the room. I left some money on the mattress for the young apprentice girl and left the room too.

192

I did not get much out of the fortune teller. I had the feeling she was expecting to hear something else from me, but she noticed I wasn't ready to tell her yet, that's why she wanted me to come back later. I wondered what was going to happen in the next couple of weeks. My guilty conscience could relax a bit for now until another disaster arose. My best bet was to drill Nejim with questions. I stopped to get baklava and other sweets and headed back home in my taxicab. I was short on meat so I called Nejim and asked him to save me some of that filet mignon. He said he would bring me some after the evening prayer. I waited for him.

Nejim showed up late that evening. We sat down talking about the house and how things shaped up after the hard work we put together here. He sensed that I had something else to ask him and waited for me to bring it up. I gradually approached the subject. I told him,

"I have the feeling that I have not heard everything from you about the child story, I feel really grieved about what happened here for that boy and for his parents, and I know your family feel partially responsible after all these years, but I have to ask you; is there something else you want to add to it? Because every time I put things together in my mind, I feel there is something missing in your story – not that I am trying to question what you have told me, but something is telling me that you have not told me everything. " He was not sure what to say; after a moment of reluctance he started to speak;

"I am sorry. I did not tell you everything at the time because I thought you might not believe me if I told you the whole story."

193

"Okay, I think the time has come, and believe me I will respect everything you say, since I am becoming part of it now as you know."

"I want to tell you that I did not hold back on you any more details on purpose."

"I know you have not."

"In ancient times, before history was written, when people lived in caves up in the mountains and when the snow covered the ridges and the plains below them, there was Muzher, a king of all kings, solid like the ice surrounding him, fearful of neither magic nor the wickedness of the underworld. He was a son of Beni Summran, the cavemen of the upper land of Mashu, the highlands of the sky where no man had challenged their supremacy before. They lived in desolate isolation and hunger and battled the cold and freezing weather for many generations. Then one day King Muzher found a spring of water, warm and sweet water unlike anything around them; they had not seen flowing water before but sheets of thick ice, as thick as the rocks beneath it. He followed the warm spring water down through the valleys and plains from the icy cold mountains to this very land. He lost the trail of the water somewhere around here. He decided to dig a hole, and the hole became a well. The well spouted with sweet and warm water coming out like a fountain, enough to fill a kingdom. The frozen land around him burst into warmth and changed the never ending winter to spring and summer. He had found the eternal source of life, he whose eyes had never seen flowing water before but sheets of ice and snow covering his homeland.

He built a dazzling palace, surrounded by magical rivers and lakes. The bad Jinns of the underworld were not pleased and decided to punish him, for he had changed their ways of life and took over their domain. Before his tribe had starved and lived in caves in the bleak freezing mountains, whereas now they ruled the land of the sweet water and were challenging the Jinns in their own realm. The Jinns decided to send the head wizard to take back their lost land. The head wizard disguised himself as a beggar and, dressed in a tattered robe, came down to the kingdom of Beni Summran. He carried his magic staff with him, the staff of all magic and power. The beggar made his way through the palace, the magical rivers, and the magical lakes, then to the source of it all, the well of sweet and warm water. He hid himself in the well and waited for Muzher to come; Muzher visited the well every evening to pay tribute to the source of his fortune."

"King Muzher noticed an unusual flickering of light in the water, and as he leaned forward to take a better look; the head wizard leaped upward and pulled him down into the water. There was a fight. Muzher with his sword, a magnificent sword made of a metal to which only the goddesses of the highlands held the secret, and decorated with impressions of his beloved rivers and lakes, and with a hilt shaped like his well. The head wizard's staff was as tall as a man and maybe and even taller, thick enough for a good grip, and ornamented by terrifying images of the underworld that could scorch the eyes just by looking at it.

There was a fight of endless might. The fight between these two masters was relentless and lasted for many days and nights. Muzher aimed at the staff, for he knew the power of this weapon in the hands of the Jinns, a master of all Jinns, the head wizard, but the staff was solid as steel and unbreakable. The two splendid weapons in the hands of their masters clashed and went at each other with venomous and persistent will. At the end Muzher thrust his sword into the heart of his mortal enemy; the head of all wizards held his staff to the last minute, but he could no longer fight back and sunk in the water of the well. Two of the Jinns came to bid their master farewell. They bowed to the king, as a sign of respect, and covered their master with the sheath of the underworld and let him rest deep in the water of the well.

King Muzher managed to pull himself out of the well with the help of his glorious sword. The well water turned bitter from that day on. The people of Beni Summran were saddened that their water and their land turned to wasteland, and they could not live there anymore. Most of Beni Summran had to return to their ancestry lands in the highlands, back to the freezing weather again and their caves. King Muzher had a long and difficult mystery illness. It wasn't long before his body gave up and his grand sword crumbled. The king of all kings passed away. The prophecy of the head wizard in a way was fulfilled, and the land returned to its old ways. The lakes turned to dust and the rivers reversed themselves back to the forbidden mountains, then stopped flowing.

Thousands of years had passed, many people came to live in this land and the legendary fight of King Muzher and the head wizard had been forgotten. But the land again made a comeback and returned to its past glory, and rivers started flowing again with sweet and warm water. It happened that a caravan trail leading between the Far East and the Near East passed right through here. The warm and sweet water was rejuvenated and came back to life. My great-grandfather of one thousand years ago, blessed be his memory, claimed the hole and built his khan on this spot. He was not aware of the past history of the well and had not heard of the legendary fight between King Muzher and the head wizard of the Jinns in the well.

When he dug out the well again and tried to put it back to use, he stumbled on a skeleton clinging to an old piece of wood. He collected the remains and the wood and buried them all in an unmarked grave somewhere around here. Many years had passed and the new owner of the well did not notice any unusual power surrounding the well. He learned to respect the well. He had a feeling that reopening the well was not welcomed by those unforeseen powers around him. He was careful not to upset the Jinns until that day when the child vanished in the well." Nejim paused.

"Nejim, this is the most fascinating story I have ever heard, straight out of the history books." Nejim was humbled and relieved at the same time. I think he felt vindicated after all the illusions and mysterious incidents of the last month.
"I want to thank you for all your help." I understood now his relentless quest to fulfill his great grandfather's spell and take it to its final conclusions, although the affair was by no means over yet. It seemed to me that we were opening a new chapter now, the final chapter of this story which had not been written yet.
"It seems that we are finally getting to the heart of the matter now."
"Yes Abu Wa'el. The same power is back and we have to do our best to put it back to rest for good."
"So what are you suggesting we do?"

197

"We have to find the head wizard's staff and destroy it. It holds the ultimate power in the right hands."

"Oh, that's why I have seen you going around the garden looking for something. and that's why you were poking the floor here inside the house too?" Nejim smiled.

"The evil power will make one last stand to get to you because you hold the key to ending the spell and finding the staff. But we have to be careful and we should show a great respect to the remains of the head wizard, if we ever find them; we should leave them as they are and take the staff only."

"I am not going to disturb anything around here; perhaps we should leave everything as is and go on with our lives."

"You are probably right but that doesn't guarantee we will be safe, you saw things are about to move in the other direction and we should be careful and firm at the same time."

"Well, I am not sure of that either."

"Maybe I should move in here with you, it makes me feel more comfortable that way."

"No I am fine alone here and I am perfectly capable of defending myself."

"As you wish, but if you change your mind let me know, I can come and stay with you overnight and leave in the morning."

"Take it from me; nothing is going to happen, anyhow nothing I can't handle." I suddenly remembered those two workers, so I asked him,

"Incidentally, have you heard again about those two workers?"

198

"No, I have not. Is there something happened here that you want to share it with me?"

"I hate to say it, but yes, last night I heard sounds right outside in the garden and when I went to the kitchen to take a look, I saw them, those two workers both standing there in the dark wearing the same working clothes they wore when they were here last time, as if they just had finished digging that hole two weeks ago." Nejim was absolutely stunned. He jumped and started pacing the floor in a very nervous way, then responded with a thick voice,

"I don't see why they would come to your house again; do you think that they might want to rob you?"

"I don't think so, I felt for a moment like it was their ghosts or images of them and they were not real, but they vanished immediately once they saw me."

"What they were doing there then?"

"I think they were checking the garden."

"I think you are right. Those were their ghosts."

"Like you were doing?"

"Yes, those were the ghosts who bowed to King Muzher at the end of the fight."

"Why would they do that and what brought them here?"

"Those were the Jinns, trying to find their great master's skeleton and his staff."

"I don't think so; you are just letting your imaginations run wild."

"I am sure of that."

"Well, I hope they didn't find it."

"Those are the same Jinns who showed up at the end of the fight with King Muzher. If they ever find the staff before we do everything is doomed. Life would not be the same again.

199

This is getting real serious; I hope you understand this new development."

"How do you know whether they are ghosts or not?"

"Ghosts have split tongues, and sometimes forklike tongues."

"That's hard to find out. I am not going to ask them that; excuse me, can I see your tongue please?"

"You are right, so for now we just have to assume that." Nejim quickly left the house. I saw him pacing the garden looking for anything unusual there. I ran after him,

"Do you know which part of the garden they were looking at?" I said,

"Come back inside and have some tea and baklava. I did not see them taking anything." He did not answer me and kept going around, and then I said,

"What makes you think it's here in the garden; it could be anywhere."

"If they were in the garden, then it must be in the garden."

"I don't want you to touch anything. You know what happened last time."

"I am not going to."

"If they knew where it was in the garden, they must have dug it out and took it away."

"Please don't say that, but you are right. I don't see a hole in the ground anywhere around here."

"If there is, we should wait for the daylight, you can not do much now, maybe Abu Sabah will help you out in the morning, but like you said we should be careful and not disturb this man again."

"I don't trust anyone, anymore, certainly not Abu Sabah."

"Why?"

"He's got a big mouth for one thing."

"An –?"

"And I don't see why he is so selective about which side of the garden he works on, look over there, he never touched that side of the garden."

"I noticed that."

"Well do you think he knows something we don't know?"

"I don't think so."

"Anyway I am so tired now, you are tired too, you better go home now," But Nejim had one thing more to say before leaving for the night,

"I want to ask you something."

"Yes, what is it Nejim?"

"You remember Umm Ali?"

"Yes I do, how she is doing?"

"She is doing fine. She is good at building those clay ovens, Tanoors. I want her to build one for you here in the backyard."

"Why?"

"You never know when you are going to need one."

"Why would I need one now?"

"Please trust me on that one."

"Oh, I see, we'll bring her here tomorrow."

"I will do that, thank you very much."

We said good night to each other and he left. I just could not sleep well that night. This house was so profoundly sacred to Nejim. Things had new meanings around me. Something was resonating inside me. I could not detach myself from this mystery; it gave me new things to focus on, but I trusted my intuitions. I hoped I would not get unexpected visitors in the middle of the night again. I was not sure how they got into the garden last time. The front fence is almost six feet high, but when I saw them vanishing into the thin air after they saw me I thought nothing would surprise me anymore. I hoped they did not have wings to fly with or a magic carpet. If they had such power then nothing could stand in their way, and nothing would prevent them from getting inside the house. That thought really startled me.

I hoped that they didn't have guns on them. From the way they reacted, it seems they didn't, at least for now, and they were more afraid of me than I was afraid of them. I decided if they should show up again I would fire my rifle and take them down. I had the right to protect myself and my property, but if they were Jinns then they would probably leave untouched. I stayed awake till the Morning Prayer call, thinking about all these stories Nejim had been feeding me with one after the other; what if they were true? Then I got too tired thinking and fell a sleep.

Chapter 15

Tanoor

I woke up early in the morning but there was no electric power. The day started hot and dusty. I checked the switch board. The grid power was out and so was the neighborhood generator power. Several hours had passed and I was still sitting in the sweltering heat. Something was wrong with the neighborhood generator for sure, I thought to myself. I wondered if he had run out of diesel fuel. I knew diesel fuel was getting very expensive and hard to come by these days. I decided to check with the owner of the local generator. As I walked down the street, I saw the electric wires on the poles were missing and some were cut down and thrown on the ground. Many men were standing on the corner and looking at the wires too. I did not recognize any of them. I asked one of the men what happened, and he said,

"Someone cut the wires down overnight."

"Why would they do that?" I asked. The man looked at me like I was from another planet, then he said,

"They sell them in local market, they fetch good money."

"I don't see the wires I strung up just a short time ago, I guess mine are gone too." My new red and blue wires were gone.

"Where do you live?" The man asked me,

"Down the road on the other side." I said,

"Oh, the doctor's house, they must done that overnight, I can't believe how desperate people are becoming, they could've been got shot, certainly I would if I saw them doing that. This is not the first time they have done that. We were about to fix ours, if you want bring new wires and we will string them up for you too." I thanked them and went back home to call Nejim. He was at my house in a few minutes. Together we went to the same store we bought the wires from last time. We bought another two new rolls and came back home. Nejim said,

"Here it happens all the time and is nothing to be bothered about. They steal anything of value even if it means they have to risk their lives while doing it."

"Life is so cheap these days." He took the ladder with him and left to meet the other men to put the wires back up again. I just didn't have the energy to go with him again in this hot day.

I wanted to be alone for a moment away from the hectic life here, a tranquil moment on my own without the madness in this house. I wanted to sit down drink a cup of coffee outside on the veranda, American coffee, and have moment of peace and quiet for myself. I had some coffee I bought from the PX store in the Green Zone. I wanted to focus on my work and make a few calls to some of the friends I had in the Green Zone. I had applied for a couple of jobs but had not got an answer back yet. One of them was to build medical clinics all over Iraq. It was with a big American construction company located outside the Green Zone. They had an office in the Mansour area. They still didn't have the go ahead to proceed with the work. This job would take me away from this madness here of this house. I was really looking forward to starting a new job. But it seemed that this job was way down the road and not available in the immediate future. More likely I would be stuck with Nejim for the time being, and this house too.

When he came back, Nejim brought with him Umm Ali. They were both carrying bags filled with dry clay and straw. I was wondering what these bags were for. He had a delighted look on his face and quickly said,

"Umm Ali went to the river bank to get fine clay, there is one spot by the river bend away on the far end of Baghdad where the water slows down and produces the best clay to build the Tanoor. We have to mix the clay with straw and let it sit overnight in a pit dug specially for that the purpose." They both went to the backyard looking for a good spot to put the new clay oven. I suggested building it next to the kitchen on the side backyard; that way it would be easy to bring the bread out of the kitchen and bake it. They both agreed. But first they had to dig a pit to mix the clay and straw. Nejim carefully went on digging a round hole less than a foot deep. I told him,

"Be careful, digging around here can be health hazard to you. You should know that by now." He looked at me and giggled,

"We don't want that to happen again, don't we?"

"No"

"You already had that experience not long time ago."

"I love to dig in here. If it was up to me I would turn the whole garden and the backyard upside down and check under every stone around here."

"Yeah, and then we have to send you to the hospital, not even the Black Hand Man can help you, or this Hudhud bones thing." He chuckled when he heard that name again. Umm Ali listened to our conversation but showed no emotion on her face. She opened the bags of dry clay and straw and started mixing them together. Nejim finished digging up the pit.

"You did not hit anything unusual while you digging?" I asked,

"If I did, I would be bouncing all over the place from excitement."

"I guess you didn't then." He put the dry clay and straw in the pit and added water to it and let it sit there.

While he was here, Nejim took a stroll in the garden looking for unusual objects or holes in the ground. He kept looking in the corners and wet spots, but he could not find anything. I was looking at him all the time from the kitchen window, I felt this guy would not give up easy and would not stop until he found whatever it was he was looking for. Finally, after one hour in the hot sun he gave up and came back inside frustrated. I told him,

"We should agree that we do not touch anything or disturb the ground and we have to wait for a sign."

"Yes Abu Wa'el, I promise." He nodded his assent reluctantly.

"I don't want you to go around with a shovel in your hand digging holes and getting in trouble; we have just had enough of that for now."

"I am not going to touch anything." I made him swear on the souls of his ancestors that he would not touch the garden when I was not around. It was an ironclad promise. I could tell from the look on his face.

"I am about to leave now. I can't take the heat anymore. You promised me, right?"

"Right" he agreed. I could not tolerate the heat here without electricity. I waited for the Wataniya, but it seemed today was one of these bad days. Sometimes we were out of the grid electricity for ten or even twenty hours straight in this hot summer. It must be over 120 degrees and inside it felt like a blazing inferno. I got in the car and drove off after I made sure that the bird had enough water; sometimes I put some ice cubes in his bathtub but they didn't last more than a few minutes in this scorching summer. I opened the window next to him and put some more food out, so he could nibble on it whenever he got hungry. I hoped Lulu was having better luck on her side of town. Nejim stayed with Umm Ali, both of them working on the clay oven together. It seemed he was happy doing that; I didn't know why, and I did not want to know anyway.

When I got there the first thing I did after greeting my favorite dog Mimi, I checked the purple coloring on Lulu's hand. It was my way of teasing Lulu these days. Lulu seemed tired to me lately. After what happened to Talib she had been withdrawn. I didn't see that luster in her eyes anymore; I hoped it was just a phase and she would come out of it very soon. I had no plans to share the things that were going on in the house with her anymore, it just seemed unfair to her. I wanted to shield her from the agony of the never-ending problems I had in the house. She already had her share of my problems and she didn't need more of the same. I did not tell her that I visited the fortune teller again. I kept it to myself; apart from anything else, the fortune teller was not much of help anyway. I sat there and relaxed in the cold air – which had become a true luxury treat these days – while she was in kitchen. I could smell the aroma of her cooking. It engulfed the entire house and leaped to my nose and then to my hungry stomach. I felt my legs were leading the way to the kitchen where she was busy with her pots and pans. I lifted the lid of one of them and dipped a piece of bread in the succulent stew, remembering my mother when I did that screaming at me and chasing me out of the kitchen. I was expecting the same from Lulu but to my surprise I was greeted with a smile and a gentle reminder that food would be served in a few minutes. She gently pushed me out of her way and put a cold drink in my hand. I asked her if she had heard from Talib; she said,

"His friend came in yesterday to collect some of the things he had in the pushcart in the driveway, I asked him about Talib and he said he is getting better and should be back to work here very soon."

"He better because parking outside is getting unbearable." The day went by in a slow and relaxing way, with none of the hectic and unexpected emergencies which became the norm in my house. We watched an old Egyptian soap opera together and had a nice meal, then around six in the evening I was on my way back home. I had to leave before it got dark. The roads were getting real bad these days; now they had checkpoints even on the Mohammad el-Qassim highway, and the traffic was backed up for miles. I got off the highway and took side roads to Palestine Road and after another hour I made it back home, tired again. I just hoped the electricity was back by the time I got there, but it wasn't. It seemed they did a good job putting up the wires again. The generator power was back later on. I checked the refrigerator to see if the grid electricity came on while I was out; it looked as if it did because I did not have slush in the freezer. Most of the time food in the freezer had to be thrown away because of the thaw and freeze cycles.

The first thing I wanted to see was what they had done with the clay oven. The pit they dug was covered by a plastic sheet. I opened it to take a peek; the wet clay was mixed with straw and had a distinctive smell to it, as if something was fermenting there. I added a little more water to it and covered it back again. The day had started badly but ended on an upbeat note for a change. I hoped things would get back to normal from now on.

Next morning Nejim and Umm Ali woke me up very early. I made a hearty breakfast for all of us before we started working on our project; I was excited to see them working on something so authentic and in the genes of all Iraqis. Umm Ali mixed the clay and straw with her bare hands until she felt it was ready. They cleaned a small area on the concrete pavement and started working their way from the bottom up in small strips of clay, curving it around and smoothing it by pressing on the sides. It was a piece of art the way she rounded the walls and smoothed the side to a perfect shape. When they finished the cone-shaped clay oven, it looked like a marvelous piece of art, about four feet high with a good size hole, a bit off-center to the front, and another small one at the bottom for ventilation. Umm Ali, as quiet as she was and as rarely as she showed any emotion, she was smiling and had a good feeling of accomplishment although she had done this job many times over before. I sensed that this one was a special one for her, and she put the pride of her trade in that clay oven today. Umm Ali was not a talkative person. During the entire day I did not hear her uttering one word, but as both cleaned up and sat for lunch, she finally made a comment. She said,

"This is my last clay oven. And I took a special interest in building it. My best wish is to see it do the job it is intended to do." Nejim quickly changed the subject, although he was clearly happy to hear her saying those few words, and said,
"The clay oven will be ready by tomorrow morning, but before we use it for real bread baking, the clay oven has to be started by burning special willow firewood in it to further dry and harden the clay."
"Where do we get the firewood from?"
"I have some at home. I will bring it over in the morning." Before Nejim was about to leave, I took him aside and told him I want to pay Umm Ali for her work; he said I shouldn't and that he would take care of that end of things. I thanked both and told them they were welcome here anytime they felt like it. I was directing my words toward Umm Ali. Nejim left with Umm Ali after they both chatted with Sabr as if he was a real person. I did not know what to cook in this clay oven but either way it was a piece of art, and seeing it built here in front of me was a real wistful experience; a thing does not have to be useful to be appreciated, its presence alone was more than enough for me. I was delighted to have one here; in the old days almost every house used to have one in the backyard for baking fresh Iraqi bread, and other cooking. The clay oven made a comeback during the sanctions era, when people were forced to bake their own bread at home.

211

Next morning both of them came over to try it out for the first time. Nejim brought with him the willow firewood, dry and ready, and as they started firing the oven a big plume of smoke billowed out of the clay oven as if it was celebrating its first tryout. The oven quickly huffed and puffed and was on its way to join the ranks of the traditional line of good Tanoors. The clay wall began to take on a dry and hard look by the time we had finished. I tapped on the side wall; it had a distinctive ringing sound to it. Both Nejim and Umm Ali stood up next to their own creation, hands crossed as if they were looking at a newborn child. Then Nejim covered the top of the oven with a piece of plywood, and both of them left without saying a word. I could not make sense of their behavior. I went inside and closed the door behind me.

Chapter 16

Mortar Attack

Many days had passed in the hot summer of Baghdad. Historically, summer time in Iraq is the time when people's sentiments flare up. Almost all the political upheavals, coups and vendettas were set off during the summer months and this year was no exception. The political climate was ratcheted up as the fiery cleric Muqtda el-Sadr inflamed the poor population with his political rhetoric. His supporters were in the streets, some brandishing their weapons and randomly setting up checkpoints on their own all around Sadr City and the surrounding areas until the US Army moved in and ran them off and opened the roads again. The favorite spot for these checkpoints was on the main street, not more than a couple hundred yards away from the house. This was one of two main entrances to the infamous city. Those cars that were trying to avoid the checkpoint took a detour right through our side road to bypass it. The road got cluttered with short-tempered drivers sitting in their cars in the hot sun, and then another checkpoint was set up right on our road to choke the traffic completely. Our road got closed up and the traffic backed up in front of the house for hours. It depended on who set up those checkpoints, sometimes the Iraqi army or police, US Army, the Sadr militia, and other times no one knows who the militia belonged to, a mix of anonymous renegade armed men wearing face masks or in army uniform randomly checking cars and taking people away. It was a very volatile situation. There wasn't a day passed without gunfire erupting from that direction. Armed skirmishes happened almost on a daily basis at that bottleneck. It was getting unbearable to a point that I could not leave the house, whether I was going out in that direction or any direction.

The neighborhood's location right at the main road to Sadr City made it into a powder keg; the hostile drivers and violence were spreading out. Getting out and in was almost impossible. I could see that the situation was about to boil over to a point where some heavy handed power was needed to control the streets and push those renegades out of here for good. Such power was only in the hands of the US Army. Finally, the cavalry had arrived and Sadr City was under a complete lockdown by the US Army. Roads were closed in and out the city. As I drove along the Qannat highway which separated Sadr City from the rest of Baghdad, I could see the US Bradley tanks manning all the entrances to the city and patrolling streets in and out of the city in this sizzling summer. The Bradley's aimed their turrets in one direction, east over the heads of this unruly city. They watched everything that came out of that sector. The brave US soldiers had complete control on the situation, and we took a long-awaited sigh of relief and relaxed a bit. Those young brave soldiers of no more than twenty years of age in this hot summer were on full alert, battling an enemy they could not see, that came in the form of suicide bombers, car bombs, and IED's. They wore heavy body armor and Kevlar in the searing heat of the 120-degree Baghdad afternoon. When I saw them right outside my house patrolling the street, I just wanted to rush out and hug one of them, but I was sure I would be shot on the spot. They were protecting people they knew nothing or little about just a few months earlier.

The violence in Baghdad was getting worse, random mass kidnappings conducted by men dressed as policemen and using brand new police SUV's were everyday affairs, many occurred during daylight, and often the bodies of the kidnapped men showed up in the streets or floating in the river the next day. These kidnappings became a huge and lucrative business, as thugs were roaming the streets looking for kids and store owners to take them for ransom; sometimes they left a written message on the front door asking people to pay or else, people had no choice but to pay. Roadside bombs and suicide bombers were everywhere all over the country. Not a day had passed without scores of people dying in the mayhem of these ruthless and inhuman acts. Mortar attacks by the Mahdi Army became a new trend and added a new dimension to the street violence. The mortars were launched from Sadr City across the Qannat highway and into nearby Baghdad neighborhoods. By the second week of August, they became more frequent and close. Each explosion shook the walls of the house; window glasses rattled, and doors jarred open in a violent way. At the beginning, it was more of a nuisance than anything else, but as they got closer and closer it became a formidable tool of terror. It started with small thud, an eerie whooshing sound followed by a moment of deafening silence and then... a loud boom. That was a form of Russian roulette game, a nerve-racking experience when you didn't know where the next shell was going to land and how close it was going to be.

I was pinned down in the house not daring to leave because the streets were unsafe. The chance that I might run into masked men shutting down the streets and checking on people was very real, while listening to the mortars landing randomly in the neighborhood was not a good option either. At night the sound of the AC-130 Gatling gun firing in a distance was astounding. It rattled the house like a huge jackhammer operating across the street, a fearful feeling but comforting to know that it was at a distance away. The nights were busy with huge explosions, mostly bombs dropped by the US Air Force not far away. But the sound and the feeling of the Gatling gun firing off is something I would never forget; its still ringing in my ears to this day when I think about it. Every night till dawn was like that during the month of August 2004, except for a short lull at dawn. Every morning I would rub the sleep out of my eyes and leap up to the highest terrace in my house to check for possible damage and survey the surrounding houses for signs of destruction; more often I found pieces of shrapnel and lead bullets scattered around.

My usual morning breakfast in the front veranda with Sabr and my ferocious looking cat was no longer feasible; my fear bested my desire for a quiet morning with nature and forced me to retire behind my brick walls with my critter comrades. I knew full well I would be safer this way regardless of the protest noises coming from the birdcage. He had ways to ensure his complaints gained my full attention. He would go on a singing strike, at least for the morning session, and then he would mellow and return back to normal by noon time, after I bribed him with a piece of his favorite food, cucumber. The cat, unbothered, went on her usual beat around the neighborhood after she got her share for the day; she had no need for someone to look after her, she was a self-sufficient animal and independent of human recklessness.

My trips across town were getting less frequent. Nejim brought in groceries for me and stayed for a while. I could see that he was getting jittery waiting but he tried not to show it. He knew he was in the zone and it was just a matter of time. I, on the other hand knew what was on his mind but could not help him. He just needed to be patient and see what was going to happen. I was more concerned with my staying here. My military ID card was about to expire by the end of the year; without that it would be hard for me to get in the Green Zone and have the leverage of protection in a worst-case scenario. So far I had not found a job and I did not know how long this situation would last. I could not go to the Green Zone and check with friends over there; even checking on that one job prospect still was not possible with the current carnage around me here. I could not go anywhere. I only managed to go to the internet café to check my e-mails. It was something I could not do without; it was my connection to the outside world. I could not miss that for more than a day or two. I took side road and parked my car far away from the café. Without the web I felt I would be completely disconnected from reality. It was a price I had pay regardless of the danger. The internet café was almost empty in the morning, which was better for me. Any crowded place these days was a perfect attack target for those suicide bombers. A packed small place with thirty or more people is quite attractive for an insurgency attack. I didn't stay there more than half hour before leaving.

On the afternoon of August 11, mortar shells were landing in my neighborhood at a rate of 6 shells an hour. I had had a sleepless night already with the overnight bombing and the eerie feeling and vibration when the Gatling gun was in action. First came the sound of that massive gun like a high-speed drill and then it was followed by the vibration and the rattling of the windows. This morning the mortar shelling was real nerve-wracking, each time I heard one coming I found myself who in the neighborhood had got that one. The day was long, filled with anticipation of the unknown. I contemplated leaving the house to go to my cousin's deep on the other side of Baghdad, but the roads were very dangerous to travel. There could be several checkpoints manned by who knows who, even the police these days were not to be trusted and they could be from any of the renegade groups. Most likely the Mahdi Army which infiltrated the police force and the Interior Ministry. If they saw a value in detaining a person, they would take that person in and sell him to the insurgents or street gangs which were roaming the streets of Baghdad unabated. In many cases hostages changed hands from one group to the other, and each time they changed hands the head price went up, like being auctioned several times over. Each person had a value on his head here in Iraq. Americans fetched the highest price as they could be sold to al-Qaeda, but after being sold and bought many times over before they get there. I fit that high price tag; having said that, I had to be very careful driving around Baghdad in such turbulent times. I weighed my options and decided to stay put rather than taking a chance in the streets. If someone tried to take a chance on me, he had to face the wrath of my lethal weapons first.

It was around four pm on that day. I was laying down in my bed half-asleep and waiting for the Wataniya to come on so I could have the AC on in the bedroom. The Wataniya was due at four; the jingling sound went off, it woke me up from my sleep. As I jumped off the bed heading out of the bedroom, I heard the dreadful whooshing sound followed by another one. I closed the door behind me, and then a big explosion, followed by another one, ripped the inside of the house. The shockwave dislodged the door off its frame and almost came flying at me and threw me on my side. The sounds of the blasts were horrific. I felt like my head was on fire from the blast. I could hear my heart pounding, I did not know if it was because I was hit by something or just the shock, but I felt something had grazed my hair from that blast. A strange miasma engulfed the house. I was gasping painfully for air. One of the blasts was in the bedroom where I was had been laying just a second ago. I ran in terror to the bathroom to look at my face in the mirror, horrified at the possibility that I was hit. Thank God my face was in one piece and no blood. I checked my body all over; I was still standing on my legs and there was no sign of blood anywhere on my body; it was just that my legs were wobbling and shaking.

As I left the bathroom I heard someone pounding on the gate. I quickly grabbed my rifle and went to take a peek from the kitchen window. I did not see anyone. I could swear I heard someone at the gate but it could be the concussion playing havoc with my senses. My head was about to explode and I had this feeling that I was numbed all over. I just did not want to think about it anymore, whoever was there they could come and take a chance with me and my rifle. The shock I felt earlier turned to rage. I cocked my weapon and put it on safety. I just hoped it wasn't one of those shadowy figures that I have seen many nights before. At that moment I was ready to empty a clip at anything entering my house, real or not real.

Inside my bedroom the ceiling fan was laying on my bed and thousands of window glass pieces sprayed all over the room – some were pitted in the bed headboard. A cloud of smoke covered the upper half of the bedroom with a distinct gunpowder-like smell. The window iron bars were mangled and blown toward the inside of the bedroom, leaving a big hole the size of a basketball in the middle. The AC unit which I just bought was dripping in oil-like liquid. The wardrobe cabinet was torn apart and the huge mirror on its side door was shattered to pieces on the floor. The second mortar shell must have landed somewhere else, it couldn't be far away and it must've been in the backyard of the house. I was in panic mode at that moment.

I truly believed I was under attack and targeted because they found out who I was. I knew Nejim would think that the evil head wizard had risen from his dormant sleep and got up from his grave and attacked me. But I just didn't have time for such nonsense. Even if he was, let him step forward, I would let him know what modern weapons could do to him. I thought by now, most of the people in the neighborhood knew who I was anyway. In my mind I thought I was in imminent danger and surely this would be followed by another attack, probably by men breaking down the front gate and marching right through my fortress; it was an "Enemy at the Gate" scenario, this was it. I could not see how two mortar shells would land in such a small backyard not more than twenty feet wide and surrounded by three-story houses on at least two sides. It must've been planned! I thought to myself, maybe that wizard was behind it after all, but how would he know about mortars, this old goon? I grabbed my AK and put on my army badge around my neck, and took a peek at the gate door again from the kitchen window. I could not see anyone. I hid myself in the corner of the kitchen waiting and listening. Ten minutes passed, then, I heard a noise in the back of the house. I thought "this is it" and I got ready for the final minutes of my life. I was determined not to go down alone.

I steadied myself on my feet, ready for anything that might come my way. As I opened the door leading to the backyard, I heard a very unusual sound, a distinctive voice; someone was shouting not in Arabic but in English, An American voice. How could that be I wondered, in my backyard? The head wizard speaks English now? As I looked, I saw three US Army soldiers were on top of the back fence, climbing from the next door house. Once I made eye contact with them, I quickly flashed my US army ID card and shouted my name and followed it up with,

"I am from Columbus, Ohio." The American voice said,
"I am Sergeant Robert from Eugene Oregon" then he said,
"What the hell are you doing here, are you okay?" I told him,
"Yes, I am okay. It just missed me by a fraction of a second. It landed here in the window, and the other one landed somewhere around in the backyard." I looked on the ground and I saw a big hole, then I said,
"It must have landed right there. This is my house and I live here." He was totally surprised to see an American here, and he said,
"I am chasing where those mortar shells had landed so we can get a good fix on the source location. We are stationed

222

in the college dormitory not far away from here. I guess they are aiming at us and keep missing."

"I did not know there was a US Army unit here."

"Yes, you can see our M1-Abram tank from the freeway."

"Yes, I have seen it, facing Sadr City."

"These are 80-mm shells." He was looking at the damage it did to the windows and outside on the ground. The new water tank I just bought was peppered with hundreds of small holes, as was the new AC unit. The electric wiring outside was shredded to pieces and even a small tree was knocked down, but the Nebga tree was there untouched. After they inspected the damage, Sergeant Robert gave me his cell phone number and asked me to give him call in case of an emergency. I felt extremely gratified and expressed appreciation for him and the others. Now I knew I had a powerful friend in case I needed help around here.

I went back inside not sure what to do. I took another look at the mess as if I was in a dream. But I thanked God for saving me one more time. Sabr was quiet; he sensed the seriousness of the situation and kept his silence. I was in a wretched state and worn out. I felt dizzy all of a sudden and my feet fell heavily; I wanted to throw up. I just collapsed on the sofa for a moment. I locked the doors then came back just to collapse on the sofa. My legs felt like jelly. I wanted to catch a moment alone and reflect on the last horrific hour. It was the after-effect of the concussion. I thought to call Lulu but then I changed my mind. I thought, I should keep it to myself for now and not have her worried about me. She would come right away, which was not a good idea under the current circumstances.

Nejim.......Nejim

Chapter 17

Umm Ali & The Jinns

After I rested for a while, I heard again someone at the gate shouting. This time it was Nejim screaming,

"Abu Wa'el, are you okay?" I answered him
"Yes, I am Nejim." I carefully went out and let him in. He had a dreadful look on his face and he was carrying a handgun.
"I don't know what I would do if something happened to you Abu Wa'el."
"They missed me by a flash of a second. The mortar shells landed in my bedroom and another one in the backyard, but both missed me by not more than a second. I just got up after I heard the Wataniya bell jingling and left the bedroom to switch the changeover when the mortar hit the bedroom window where I was just a second before."
"Allah was with you, God is Great, God is Great. I have been prying for your safety since you got here Abu Wa'el; you know how much that means to me."
"Yes, I do Nejim, everything is alright."
"Is the bird okay?"
"Yes he is okay too."
"Do you mind if I go and take a look at him."

"No, go ahead." I was fully absorbed by the destruction inside the house. I went inside the house to take another look at the bedroom and count my blessings. Someone upstairs was looking after me at that moment. The timing of the Wataniya was something beyond explanation. It was just a matter of seconds between life and death. If I was still in my bed just one second longer, I would have been ripped to pieces; not only that, the falling of ceiling fan would have cut me apart. I looked at the spray of glass pieces embedded in the headboard just where my head would've been, that could've been my face, I thought to myself.

I went to the kitchen to see Nejim; he had the birdcage on the floor and he was sitting crossed-legged in front of it, almost crying and reciting some religious phrases as if the bird was some sort of deity. The bird seemed to be responding to him and looking straight down, sometimes sideways, but always quiet. Nejim did not see me, and I quietly stepped back and left the kitchen. I was going to say something while I watched such odd behavior but I thought whatever I said that moment would rebound without making contact with him. He was completely taken, and almost subconscious, transcending to another world, a world of his own. I settled to leave him in his secluded thoughts. I opt to revisit that matter on a more appropriate moment. The house was in a big shambles, not one window glass had stayed undamaged. I felt lightheaded and my legs were about to give in. I had to rest. The sofa in the living room was the safest place in the house to lay down on right now, fearing more mortar attacks. Nejim came over with a cold water bottle and sat next to me,

"I need to ask something Nejim."

"Yes, Diktor."

"Please stop calling me Diktor, because, I am not."

"Okay Stadd Saad."

"Just call me Abu Wa'el."

"Yes Abu Wa'el."

"I need to ask you a question."

""What is it?""

"What was the name of that child who disappeared long time ago?" There was a long pause, and I did not know whether to ask the question again or not. I looked at him in the eye, waiting for an answer from him.

"Well?" then he said,

"It was Sabr" I almost fell off the sofa when I heard that.

"How could it be?"

"It's been written Abu Wa'el. This is the course of history. We are witnessing the last chapter of this legacy being unraveled right in front of our own eyes and we are part of it."

"How did I know when I called him that, it just came to me, it was not like a name I heard so many times before and I wanted to call this bird by it?"

"It's been written Abu Wa'el; you had no say in that. You have to believe in this destiny, it's not only my destiny or my family's, it's yours too."

"Am I suppose to believe that this bird's name is the same as the child's who disappeared long time ago? You knew all along that this bird is that child."

"Yes Abu Wa'el."

"When did you know that?"

"When you showed him that feather you carried in your pocket, and he went wild about it."

"Why he went wild when he saw the feather?"

"Because it belonged to his mother."

"But how did you know about those two birds? I never told you about them."

"You didn't have to; I sent them to your house.'

"I don't believe anything you are saying right now; it must be all a dream."

"It could be a dream; we all live in the shadows of our dreams. Life and death is a dream." I immediately remembered my dream when he said that.

"What is going to happen now?"

"The evil spirits, the Jinns are still hard at it. They are after you and we saw what happened just now. That was not an accident, it was a sign. It happened because they wanted it to happen, but I am here to protect you. You remember how much I wanted to add the light and the ring sound to the electric changeover panel?

"Yes I do."

"There was a purpose to that."

"That jingle sound saved my life."

"Yes Abu Wa'el, do you believe me now?"

"I am ashamed to say, I do finally. There are many things now that are falling into place and making sense, many signs as you say." I said that but I was not fully convinced myself. I wasn't sure of anything around here anymore. It could be no more than incredibly convincing coincidences and close calls. The thrust of the events besieged my thoughts. I wanted very much to know where we were going from here on. Nejim said,

"We have to wait for another sign. You will know when it comes." As if what happened today was not a good enough sign for whatever we need to do next."

"It is getting close."

"Yes Abu Wa'el. It could be today and we have to be ready. They have tried once but they failed."

"After the mortar attack, I thought I heard someone at the gate but when I looked outside, I did not see anything."

"Those are the ghosts, perhaps checking on you."

"But I did not see anyone."

"Sometime you don't see them in the daylight."

"Are you telling me they could be here now and we cannot see them?"

"No Abu Wa'el, they won't dare to enter your house, they are scared as much as we are, but they will do their best and we should not underestimate them."

"I am really tired now."

"Get some sleep and I will be here all the time. I will not leave you, not for one moment. I am going to call my son to fetch Umm Ali and get her here."

"Why?"

"Umm Ali is a powerful woman in the world of Jinns, the good Jinns. She can block any curse or unseen spirits from entering the house or doing any harm. She is resolute and committed to the cause. "

"Is she like Umm Murad?"

"No she is not a fortune teller, but she has her own ways."

"Does she know about this thing too?"

"Absolutely, Abu Wa'el. She is a woman of strong means, and she has been with us for a long time, but that's another story."

"What other story?"

"Well, she has ways to find out things no one would know about."

'Go and get her. I want to talk to her too. I can use all the help I can get."

"You remember when we visited her house?"

"Yes I do."

"You remember the empty birdcage, you kept looking at in her house."

"Oh yes I remember the birdcage, and those two Bulbuls outside the cage."

Those are Sabr's parents, the ones who came to visit you in the garden."

"Oh, okay whatever."

"She has been taking care of them. They are the ones who alerted me about you."

"I see."

"They are waiting too for the day to end the one thousand year spell."

"I am sure."

"One thing I want to tell you, Umm Ali can't come alone, it's Meharam, and we are two men in the house. She has to bring her son Ali with her too.'

"That's no problem, they can sleep in the bedroom upstairs and we sleep downstairs, I will be in the other bedroom facing the backyard, and you can sleep on the sofa here looking at the front yard."

"That's great, thanks."

"I wanted to ask you longtime ago, but could not find the right time to do that."

"Okay, today is the right time to ask anything you want."

"When I visited you in your house, I saw a piece of stone in your bedroom covered by a green velvet piece of cloth, what was   that?"

"It's one of the stones that went into the well one thousand years ago when my great grandfather the lodge keeper decided to fill the well with stones. We have it in our family for generations."

"Okay I figured that."

"Why don't you get a little sleep for now Abu Wa'el."
"Yeah I reckon I need it." I went to sleep and Nejim waited
for Umm Ali and her son to show up.

Around six in the evening, Umm Ali arrived with her son and
Karrar. I showed her the room upstairs. I noticed that she was
carrying a thick pole which had a big ball of solid black tar on
one end. It was some sort of medieval club, like Iraqis used in
the old days. I asked Nejim about it, he said,

"It's a Megwar."
"What is it for?"
"It's for crushing those ghosts, if they ever show up."
"I want to see that, but what's wrong with using a good old
AK-47 rifle."
"Abu Wa'el, that's the way we do it here, leave it to Umm
Ali, she is a diva in these things. She is perfectly capable of
handling herself."
"You have great confidence in Umm Ali."
"I sure do, and I speak from experience." I felt I was way
overwhelmed today. Now I had a medieval army to protect
me. I just needed Lulu here and Mimi with me so I could sleep
better tonight and with confidence.

Umm Ali went on preparing dinner for us, and we all sat down
afterward watching TV. I kept looking at the other bedroom
but dared not to go inside. I just didn't have it in me to go in
there. The room door was on the floor, broken up, and I didn't
even bother to push it aside. Nejim took it off and set it aside,
he said,
"I will have people come in and fix everything up including
the window glasses. I will take a look at the AC unit; maybe

231

we can salvage it, but let's finish this business first. I think by tomorrow everything will be clear."

"I hope we will make it tonight."

"We will." Nejim went in the kitchen and covered Sabr with a towel,

"I want to keep him quiet for tonight."

"Oh, and keep that cat away from him; one way I do that is by feeding her real good so she won't have any desire to feed on him."

"She will not bother him."

We all went to bed around midnight after the power went out. I went to bed and left the windows open to the backyard. I kept my favorite short AK rifle next to my bed. I was tossing around all night. The sound of bombing was far away tonight and less bothersome, but I had something else on my mind. Finally I shut my eyes. Hours later I felt that something was in the room with me, a whiff of a breeze like when someone had just passed by me in the dark. I woke up and looked at my watch, it was around four in the morning; as I turned around I saw the shadow of a man looking at me in the window. I jolted off my bed but he quickly disappeared. I got up and walked up to the window. There were two men digging again in the backyard. They must have been not more than twenty feet away from the window. I thought this time they are not going to get away. I ran back to get my rifle, but I saw Umm Ali and Nejim standing there followed by Ali. Umm Ali was ready with her stout club in her hand; she looked like a warrior ready for her lifetime combat. Nejim signaled to me to open the kitchen door. I got the key and we all left the room,

"I can take them down now." I said,

"That's not going to do it Abu Wa'el."

"Why is that?"

"There is only one way to finish them off, and Umm Ali knows how to do it. She's been getting ready for this moment for a long time. It's her moment to shine." I felt I was about to witness a historical battle between good and evil in a traditional sense.

"Okay, I want to see this." I opened the kitchen door and let Umm Ali out, as if I was letting a pitbull dog out to the dogfight arena. She had her hair looped and tucked under a black Charghad, a loose black cloth wrapped around the head. She put the end of her black gown between her teeth and held it tight as she revealed black and thick long socks; she was all black on black from head to toe. She pushed her slippers aside and clinched her awesome black club high in both hands. She was ready to take on those two men. I let her out and whispered in her ears,

"Go Get'm Tiger." Both of us quickly ran back to the window to watch what was going to happen, as if we were about to witness gladiators clashing for the fight of their lives. I grabbed my rifle just in case I needed it, or maybe Umm Ali needed an extra hand.

Umm Ali dashed out at the men with a confident stride, but she did it deliberately and quietly, as if she was a cat about to leap on her prey; she held the club high on one side like a Samurai warrior. When she approached them both men got up; one had a shovel and the other one a pickaxe. She took a powerful swing at the one with the shovel but he blocked the blow, then she turned around at lightning speed and looped the pickaxe loose from the hands of the other man. The pickaxe

233

went up in the air and landed far away; then she rammed the man in the chest with her club and took the last gasp out of his breath. He fell back and hit his head hard on the side brick wall and went down with pain. She stepped back for a second and raised her club again and poised her hands and grabbed hard on the lower end of the club, then charged at the first man. I could almost see the terrified look on his face. Umm Ali landed a big blow from her club right on his forehead; she must have crushed his skull with that blow. The man almost flipped in the air and went down. Then both men got up on their feet again, but they were staggering like two drunken men. As she was contemplating a second attack, a bright light shot down from the Jujube tree and touched the heads of both men, and both men vanished completely into the tree. They must have awakened the entire population of those noisy crickets in the tree, because they just went on a wild chirping and would not quiet down until that mysterious light was quenched forever.

That was a spectacular fight, and it all happened right here in front of my eyes. Umm Ali set them up like a stealthy ancient warrior; she walked out from the dark of the night and took those two men by surprise and consigned them to oblivion. They froze and did not have time to get themselves together and counterattack or use any of their Jinn's power. It ended as swiftly and as fast as it started, with two lethal blows.

As the fight finished, we heard the Morning Prayer call blaring in the dark night. Umm Ali turned around and looked at us in a triumphant way. Nejim went crazy shouting "Allah O Akbar", "God is Great", then he was chanting "Ma Itjeebha

Illa Neswanha", Only our women would take care of things; he was dancing with joy and excitement.

Chapter 18

Free at last

Umm Ali came back inside the house poised and smiling. She said,

"We don't have to worry about them anymore; they are cursed now and for good. They have turned into two Abu Feswa's, the tree crickets." The three of them cleaned up and got ready for their morning prayers. When they finished, Umm Ali fired up the clay oven outside with the firewood Nejim had brought with him from home. Umm Ali and I sat next to the clay oven looking at the blazing fire, then she said,

"I have made "Khubuz el-Abbas", Abbas bread ready to celebrate the occasion." She went on and started baking the bread in the clay oven as the sunlight started to come out.

We went outside in the back of the house to look at the damage the mortar shells did to the windows and the backyard. The new water tank and AC unit were both useless. All the windows were shattered. The house needed a complete overhaul again, but the best part of it was that I was still alive and no one got hurt. We found a big hole in the ground where the second shell landed. Nejim said,

237

"That's where those guys were digging." he started pushing aside some of the overgrown plants surrounding the hole.

"That's right. " I said. As we were talking; we heard another whooshing sound coming this way. We hurried back inside the house and hid under the stairwell. This time, I did not want to take a chance near a window or a door. The mortar shell landed on the other side of the neighborhood, probably near the food distribution center. I still wanted to take a second look at that spot, and Nejim and Umm Ali showed keen interest in the hole.

"Why were those two men digging there? Before, they were interested in the front garden; now they shifted their attention to the backyard and in that part of the backyard."
"This must be it; they know where to find the head wizard's staff. It must be buried there for sure." Nejim said.

We went back again to check out the hole. It was hidden in the shrubs of that mean plant. The hole was about three feet wide and another one or two feet deep. Umm Ali was the first to push the soil aside with her bare hands, going deeper in the hole. Then all of a sudden she stopped digging while her hand was still in the hole. Nejim leaped over her shoulder to take a look; I backed off a few steps, just to be on the cautious side. It seemed she had found something there. Nejim said,

"What is it?"
"I don't know yet." She answered.
"Can you feel it?" I said,
"It's heavy. " I thought it could be a piece of the mortar shell, I immediately said,

"Leave it there and don't touch it again, it could be a live piece of that mortar shell." Nejim said,

"Maybe not. "

"We should not take a chance on it. This is a serious business, it could explode, or something." Umm Ali pulled her arm out of the hole.

"Did you touch something?" I asked her.

"I touched something hard with the tip of my finger."

"Was it metal or wood?" I asked her again.

"I couldn't tell; it just had a strange feeling."

"The mortar shell exploded, and these are some of the pieces scattered around."

"I am not so sure about that, let's not take a chance on it."

"Those two men were digging here and it seemed they were not bothered about it."

"We should not do the same thing just because those two men were doing it."

"Okay Abu Wa'el."

"Look what happened to them; they are not exactly your average human beings" I said again.

"Yes let's do that," he said.

We went back inside the house. I wanted to leave whatever she had found where it was and bury it. I had had enough surprises in this house. I did not want to take chances and have someone hurt, but those two guys smelled blood and they were like hound dogs on a trail. I realized whatever I said, it would not sway them to change their minds. It was a big safety and moral dilemma to me. I knew myself. I was not going to be anywhere near that hole once they start digging it out. Whatever she found there was none of my concern, but at the same time I did not want anyone else to get hurt unnecessarily.

239

"I am thinking to call Sergeant Robert and have him come and take a look at that hole first, before we do some more digging."

"Abu Wa'el, please let's take care of it ourselves, it means so much to us and our cause." Nejim and Umm Ali would not hear any of it. When I asked them why, Nejim said,

"We are very sure that the head wizard's staff is buried there."

"How could you be so sure?"

"Although Umm Ali just barely touched it, she felt the grip on the staff, she knows."

"Okay let's go and take another look at it, but you have to promise me not to touch anything."

"I will Abu Wa'el" We looked around the hole and in the shrubs we found the remains of a finlike tail of the mortar shell. Nejim was ecstatic,

"Now I am sure that that mortar exploded when it hit the ground, and there is nothing left of it in the hole."

"Okay let's plan this first, let's assume that is the staff of the head wizard, and Umm Ali is going to try to get it out, right."

"Yes"

"And what's next? You told me that you cannot look at the staff, right?"

"Yes."

"So how are you going to deal with that?"

"I brought with me the green velvet, I will wrap it around the staff so we don't look at or touch it, and Umm Ali will take it to the clay oven and burn it."

"What about the bones?"

"If there are bones there too, I promise that we will not touch them and will leave them where they are and re-bury them if needed." I was still not convinced that that old piece of wood was actually here, and at the very least I wanted to be careful.

Umm Ali left to restart the fire in the clay oven again. Nejim was psyching himself up for this long-awaited moment; he was pacing the floor back and forth and making everybody nervous. For Nejim and his family, this was a historical event. This was a remarkable moment that they have been waiting for generations; it was very personal and contained many of the aspirations his family had passed on from father to son. I myself just wanted to get this thing over with in a peaceful way. When both were ready for their big moment, I kept a comfortable distance just in case of explosions or any unexpected mishaps, in fact I was inside the house, in the bedroom, looking over the backyard from the window. I hoped that the old wizard would not rise from the dead and devour everyone in sight. They first went on cutting all the shrubs surrounding the hole and cleared up the loose soil around it, then Umm Ali started digging again with her bare hands, very carefully piling up the soil on the side of the hole. Nejim was terribly anxious and looking over her shoulders. I really wanted him to stay away from the hole, but whatever I said right now to him was not going to make a difference; but I was worried that he might be making her nervous, and second I really didn't want him to get blown up too. In my mind I wasn't fully convinced of what they were after. But that was irrelevant now. Anyway it was his funeral.

Suddenly Umm Ali stopped digging, but her hand was still in the hole holding something, Nejim quickly asked her,

"What is it?"

"I am not sure yet. It's something hard; I can feel it but I can't get a grip on it."

"Dig around it first, and don't pull hard on it." I yelled from behind the window. I ran to get her a little garden spade I had from the storage room. She started digging and hauling soil out of the hole, then she reached inside the hole with Nejim looking over her shoulders again. Then she said,

"I think I found it." Nejim screamed,

"How does it feel?"

"It's like a piece of wood, a very hard and smooth wood." Then I said,

"Try to dig along the staff; don't try to nudge it out yet." She kept going on it and every once in a while felt the staff.

"Can you feel the end of it."

"I can feel one end but the other one is too far deep in the ground." Then Nejim said,

"Maybe we can pull it out from one end, but try to nudge it loose first."

"You need to get that sacred cloth ready."

"I have it here with me." Nejim answered, and then he reached inside his pocket and got it out, and kissed it and touched his forehead with it in reverence.

"Here we go; I am going to pull it out now, get ready." Nejim was getting ready to spread the sacred cloth over the staff when it was coming out of the ground. While he was doing that, the crickets in the Jujube tree started a horrible chorus, a shrieking intense sound. Some of these crickets left the Jujube tree and dropped down on the ground and started gathering together in a very threatening way. I was immediately struck by their presence on the tree and their number dotted about on the ground. They were invisible just a moment earlier; now they were everywhere.

"This is not a friendly tree" I loudly complained to myself. "Neither are those critters." I was appalled at the Jujube tree's behavior. I thought it was a friendly tree and we were friends. How could she treat us so carelessly and harbor those little monsters with creepy looks and shameless intentions among her branches?

"Jujube you are no friend of mine." I said. But those crickets did not heed my plea and kept coming at Umm Ali first. Ahead of the crowd were two black ones with blaring fiery eyes almost popping out of their sockets, and a mouth full of shiny dancing teeth. They sure looked formidable for their own little creepy size, but their comfort was in number and they did have a considerable number around us by now. I had to do something. This was not a friendly gathering. I had to think quickly and react even quicker. Umm Ali let go of the staff and immediately those bloodthirsty critters calmed down and started to back off, reversing their early uncompromising hostile posture. They quickly started hopping up to the comfort of their tree and almost disappeared in its thicket.

"Let's stop and think this over for now, we are in no rush." I clearly was frustrated, so was everyone else except Umm Ali; she never showed any emotion, solid like a rock. The only time I saw her smiling was when Nejim whispered in her ears something about me the first time we met. But that felt like such a long time ago, and it did not matter anymore. "Let's take a tea break." Nejim said quietly.

243

"Make sure to push the loose soil back in the hole, so we don't arouse those obnoxious creatures again." Umm Ali rushed out to do that. I quietly told Nejim,

"We need to improvise a plan to catch those demons before they get on the ground."

"They know when the staff is about to come out."

"It seems the staff triggers their moves."

"There must be something we can do."

"Did you look at those big black ones?"

"Yes, and their big eyes and dancing shiny teeth. I have the feeling that those two black big dudes are those two workers. They simply converted to two of those nasty crickets."

That's the second time they did that."

"We just have to do what we have to do, and be ready for what comes after." Umm Ali said,

"I am ready, I will take the staff and run with it to the Tanoor; once it's there, it's over."

"Okay, we have to do it at lightning speed."

"Tewekelu ala Allah; put your trust in God."

Umm Ali went back to the hole again, digging in a frantic way before those mean creatures woke up again. Whatever Umm Ali did today, she did it like she meant it and with great confidence. Nejim was behind her with that magic piece of cloth. She grabbed the end of the staff and started pulling it out, but then stopped dead and looked up at the tree. I was there too daring those devils from climbing down the Jujube tree, but as before they started dripping down with a ringing sound every time one of them hit the ground, then the drip became a gush, more than I could count. They were on the ground and heading in one direction. Then a pair of black-cheek Bulbuls hovered above our heads. Umm Ali seemed to know them; she exchanged glances with them, and she had a confident look on her face, as if she knew what these two birds were up to. No more than a minute had passed before a flock of Bulbuls burst on the scene from nowhere, and swooped down on the tree in military precision and landed, glaring at those evil creatures down below. They were like a regiment of warriors marching to battle. The ill-fated crickets looked up above their heads and knew what was coming their way. Abu Feswa crickets are the bulbul's favorite meal, not to mention their mortal enemies for today. Hundreds of Bulbuls took off again and soared above in the sky, then dove straight down in a final crescendo at their unfortunate foes. Those crickets could do nothing about it but wait for their inevitable demise. The head of the flock aimed at those two black ones first and tore them to pieces. They sunk their beaks in their crests and crunched them head first with a crackling noise. The Bulbuls gorged themselves on the feast and before too long it was all over. The flock of birds disappeared as fast as they had appeared in the sky above the house.

Umm Ali carefully woke up the staff from its deep sleep, a magnificent piece of art worthy of all admiration. I wanted to feel it, caress the carvings and the images, and say a final good bye to it. I wanted to run my fingers over the skin of this sleeping monster and feel the trembling power it held. It finally dawned on me that I might be able to do that without incurring its wrath. I asked Umm Ali,

"Slow down; I want to have a feel of it." Nejim quickly objected,
"La, No Abu Wa'el, don't get closer to it please."
"Don't worry; I am not going to look at it."

245

"Let me cover it first." He brought in the piece of cloth and quickly dropped it on the staff." I touched it and moved my hand on top of the deep grooves in the wood, sensing it, and hunting for clues in my mind, the meaning of the mystery. I could feel a strange vibe emitting from the depth of the lines under my fingers. It was an image of a head of some sort; that much I could tell. I had an urge going down my soul to take a look at this forbidden image, an image I suddenly craved to see. I felt the sensation coming through the wood and I was in another world completely. I did not hear or feel anything else, Nejim was screaming at me and shaking me violently while I was about to reveal the secret and remove the cloth,

"Abu Wa'el, Abu Wa'el don't do it." I was in a transcending dream; I felt everything stood still around me. I gripped the staff hard while my sweat was pouring right down my nose and chin. Then I let it go.

"I am okay Nejim." It was a beast; it carried a potent power even after thousands of years and would not go down without a fight. Unearthing such foe took some doing. We did not look but I was sure it sensed the end as it slipped out of its rest. It was tall and heavy and had a commanding presence. Nejim was quick, draping it with his cloth from one end to the other. They both rushed it to the Tanoor and shoved it into the flaming core. A howling flame with a roaring sound billowed out. I saw the flames of fire dancing restlessly. The ground rumbled under our feet and the door of the birdcage flew open. Sabr took off and perched on my shoulder, singing and dancing. We were both looking at the clay oven. Umm Ali was battling a thundering flame and pushing the remains of the burning staff into the mouth of the Tanoor and yelling at the fire to finish off the beast.

Nejim left the scene serenely, followed by Sabr, and trailed by my cat and the other two Bulbuls flying just above his head. I knew where they were going. I looked toward the front of the house and saw the front gate tilting to one side, the side where the water had gushed out of that terrible hole in the ground. I too ran toward the gate. I did not want to miss that moment for anything, the end of the epic finally at hand. The earth gaped below us, right where that hole had stood before. Sabr flew back into the hole. It was a moment of silence. A score of people gathered outside, and then even some more, astounded at what was happening; some wanted to know, and some already knew, among them Lulu and I, overjoyed and pleased. Thirteen birds came out of the hole, fluttering their wings for the first time in one thousand years. They flew off into a clear sky with an army of other birds waiting for them to celebrate life again after all these years. They turned around and dipped their wings on one side as a final salute and appreciation to those who had carried the burden of their cause. We could see the face of the child printed high in the heavens, smiling down on us. I turned to Nejim and Umm Ali; they were both profoundly happy. Finally, Nejim and his ancestry had fulfilled their own sense of destiny, the destiny they had all sought after for all these years.

The End

Nejim.......Nejim

A Glossary of Arabic Words and Phrases

Nejim   نجــم
A common Iraqi name meaning stars.

Mustansiriya District   حـــي المستنصـــرية
A residential area around the Mustansiriya University.

Sadr City   مدينـــة الصــدر
A poor residential area east of Baghdad.

el-Thawra   الثـــورة
The old name of Sadr City.

Abdil Kareem Qassim   عبــد الكــريم قاســم
The Prime Minister of Iraq, 1958-1963.

Muqtada el-Sadr   مقتــدى الصــدر
A youing Shiite clergyman who started the Sadr movement.

Qanat Highway   طــريق القنــاة الســريع
A highway separating Sadr City and the rest of Baghdad.

Ameriya District   حـي العامريــة
A residential area around the highway links the airport and
 Baghdad.

Rasheed Hotel   فنــدق الرشــيد
A hotel located on the northwest tip of the Green Zone.

249

Tahrier Square ساحة التحرير
The main square in downtown Baghdad.

Wareqa ورقة
Wareqa means leave, but it's the Iraqi lingo for the $100 bill.

Chapter 2
Hurriya City مدينة الحرية
Another poor residential area northwest Baghdad.

Shou'ella City مدينة الشعلة
Another poor residential area northwest Baghdad.

Qadisiya complex مجمع القادسية
A high-rise building within the Green Zone.

Karada كرادة
An old neighborhood along the east side of Tigris River.

Chiffiya كفية
The traditional Arab head cloth men wear.

Dishdash دشداشة
The traditional Arabic dress men wear.

Chapter 3
Kiayatt كيات
A KIA minibus.

Coasterat كوسترات
A Toyota medium size bus.

Sha'ab City   مدينــة الشــعب
A poor residential area north of Sadr City.

Hawasim   حواســم
A nickname to the looting occurred after the fall of Baghdad.

Diktor   دكتــور
Doctor.

Lalatt   لالات
Oil lamps.

Ghassab   قصــاب
Butcher.

Mohammad el-Qasim Highway طــريق محمــد القاســم الســريع
A highway east of Baghdad.

Abu Afif   ابــو عفيــف
A well known sweat store in Baghdad.

Rubbayi street   شــارع الــربيعي
A well known street east of Baghdad.

Kehraman Square   ســاحة كهرمانــة
A main square in Baghdad.

Chapter 4
Abu Nuas   أبــو نــؤاس
A famous street along the east side of the river.

Ferdous Square   ساحة الفردوس
A main square were Saddam status was toppled down after the
fall of Baghdad.

Rasheed Military Base   قاعدة الرشيد العسكرية
An old military base south of Baghdad.

el-Sadoon Street   شارع السعدون
A main street in Baghdad.

Arack   عرق
The traditional alcoholic beverage.

Sedara   سدارة
Old style military cap.

Feles   فلس
The lowest coin currency, 1000 Feles equal one Iraqi Dinar.

Elweya   علوية
A neighborhood around Ferdous Square.

Abaya   عباءة
Traditional Iraqi robe.

Umm el-Abaya   ام العبايـة
An old Iraqi song about a lady wearing Abaya.

Chapter 5
Nebga   نبقة
Jujube Tree.

Melek   ملك
A supernatural being in Iraqi mythology. Also it means king.

Abu Feswa   ابـــو فســـوة
A tree cricket makes a fart sound. Feswa means fart.

Mashi   ماشـي
Okay.

Inshalah   انشـــــالله
God's Will, most used phrase by Iraqis.

Ammara   عمارة
A southern province.

Nasirya   ناصـــرية
A southern province.

Batawiyin   بتـــــاوين
A neighborhood in old Baghdad.

Chapter 6
Hissa el-Tamwiniya   الحصـــة التموينيـــة
The food ration distributed by the government during the
 sanctions period.

Deggat   دكات
Tattoos.

Tanoor   تنـــور
The traditional old design clay oven to bake bread.

Chapter 7

Baghdad el-Jedidda بغـداد الجديـدة
A neighborhood in southeast Baghdad.

Stadi سـتاذي
The loose translation is "My Teacher", but it is used out of
 respect as in Sir.

Yekhra يقـرى
The loose translation as in "He Can Read" but in Iraqi lingo
 when used to describe Bulbul birds, it means "He Can Sing".

Bubul بلبــل
A singing bird indigenous to Iraq, Persia, and Afghanistan.

Arrasat عرصـات
Affluent neighborhood south of Baghdad.

Chapter 8

Belediya بلــديات
Local Municipality.

Ammi عمي
Uncle.

Chapter 9

Fatahelfal فتاحـة فـال
Fortune Teller.

Ammana garage market area كراج أمانة
Local market place.

Fahdel   فضـــل
Old neighborhood in old downtown Baghdad.

Shewakah   شـــواكة
Old neighborhood in old downtown Baghdad.

Shenasheel   شناشـــــيل
Old second floor Bay Window.

Chapter 10
Khan   خان
Old Travel lodge.

Muezzin   مؤذن
The caller to pray.

Chapter 11
Palestine Road   شـــارع فلســـطين
A main road east of Baghdad.

Dawoodi District   حـي الـداوودي
A Baghdad neighborhood on the west side of Baghdad.

Nahdim Ghzar   نـاظم كـزار
A notorious Chief of the Iraqi Police Intelligence in early 70's
  killed by Saddam in 1973.

Abu Tubar   ابـو طـبر
A ruthless serial killer terrorized Baghdad in early 70's called
  Abu Tubar, Hatchet Man.

Bazaz   بـزاز

Bazaz Administration A Prime Minister of Iraq in 1966.

Chapter 12

Chapter 13

Bekhoor   بخـور
Burning incense.

Defla Plant   نبـــات الدفلـــة
Rhododendron plant.

Abu Eid el-Sawdda   ابـو ايـد السـودة
Black Hand Man.

Elboushja Mosque   مسـجد البوشـجاع
A landmark mosque in karada area.

Seyedna   سـيدنا
A religious title reserved to those who are descended of Imam Ali (SAWS).

Hinna   حنـة
Dye coloring plant.

Barak Al'lah Beek   بــارك الله بيــك
Equivalent to God Bless you.

Hudhud   هدهد
Middle East Mockingbird.

Chapter 14

Jinn   جـني
A supernatural being in Arabic mythology, it can be evil or
 good.

Khatoon   خـاتون
Madam in old Iraqi lingo.

La   لا
No.

Chapter 17
Meharam   محرم
Forbidden.

Megwar   مكوار
Club.

Ma Itjeebha Illa Neswanha   ماتجيبهـــا الا نســـوانها
Only our women would take care of things.

Charghad   جرغد
An old Iraqi word describing a piece of black cloth women
used to wrap their head with during field work.

Chapter 18
khubuz el-Abbas   خـبز العبـاس
Abbas Bread, a traditional Iraqi celebratory bread.

Allah O Akbar   الله اكــبر
God is Great.

Tewekelna ala Allah   توكلنـــا علـــى الله

Nejim.......Nejim

We put our trust in God.

Chief Characters

Nejim	نجـم	The main character.
Lulu	لولـو	A distant cousin.
Mimi	ميمـي	A lovely Tibetan Spaniel dog.
Janan	جنـان	Lulu's sister.
Lamia	لاميـة	Lulu's sister.
Emad	عماد	An Iraqi translator working in the Republican Palace.
Talib	طالـب	A street peddler.
Karrar	كـرار	Nejim's son.
Sabr	صـــابر	

The wonder White-cheek Bulbul.

Umm Murad	ام مراد	The fortune teller.
Umm Ali	ام علـي	A widow.
Ali	علـي	Her son.
Jinns	جنـي	spirits; they can be evil or good spirits.
King Muzher	الملك مـزهر	A mythological king.

Neighbors

Dr. el-Hadithi	الحـــديثي
Metwal	متولـــي
Hamadani	حمـداني
Najafi	نجفـــي
Samerrai	ســـامرائي

259

Nejim…….Nejim

Baghdad

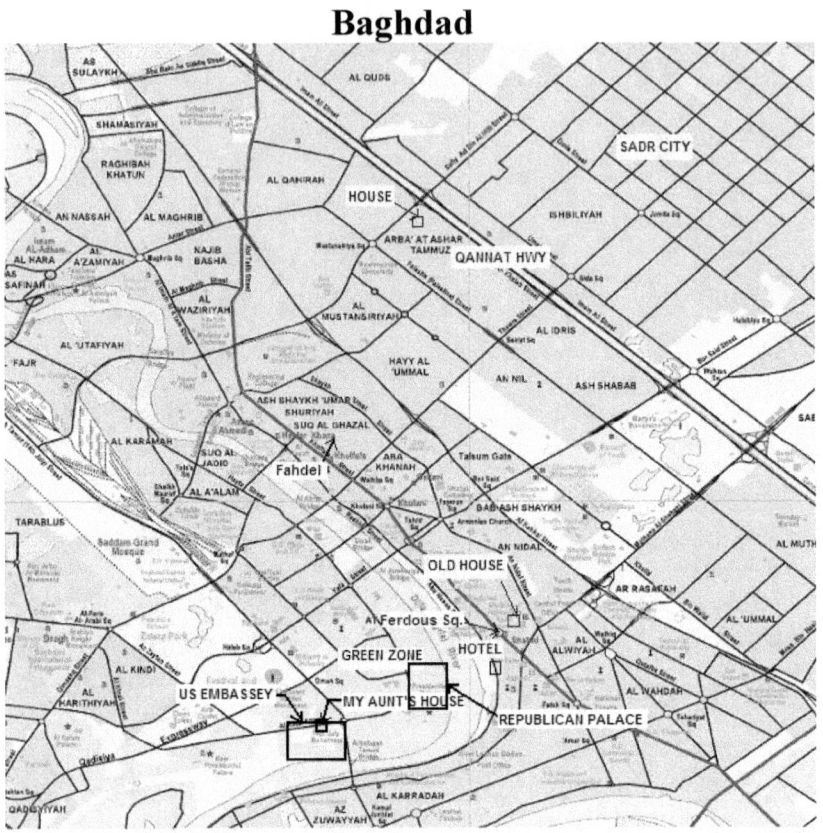

Iraq

Nejim……..Nejim

About The Author

Saad Farage was born in Iraq in 1951. He immigrated to the United States in 1976. He obtained a Master's degree in geotechnical engineering from Georgia Institute of Technology and worked as an engineer for various US engineering companies. He was part of the political oppositions to Saddam, and served with the US Department of Defense in Iraq for two years after the fall of the Baath party regime in Iraq. He has written numerous short stories about Iraq. His first novel, *The Spirit of Mesopotamia*, was about the marsh Arabs of southern Iraq. It was published in 1999. He has other books in the making, including a geotechnical engineering book, *Consulting Geotechnical Engineering & Practice*.

Nejim.......Nejim

Sabr

MiMi

265